THE OUTLAW BREED

You could smell violence in the valley when a hill man rode down through it.

War hung heavy in the air—between the rich ranchers and the wild, lawless tribe who squatted above them—and Jesse Craven was caught in the middle.

He was ramrod of the valley's biggest spread.

He was born to the hills' most savage mongrel clan.

He had a terrible choice to make—and a woman made it for him.

THE OUTLAW BREED

D. B. Newton   1916-

(Dwight Bennett)

GUNSMOKE

This hardback edition 2001
by Chivers Press
by arrangement with
Golden West Literary Agency

Copyright © 1955 by Fawcett Publications, Inc.
Copyright © renewed 1983 by D. B. Newton
Copyright © 2001 by D. B. Newton in the British Commonwealth

All rights reserved

ISBN 0 7540 8139 7

British Library Cataloguing in Publication Data available

```
38212003830665
Main Adult Western
N                    AUG    2002
Newton, D. B. (Dwight
Bennett), 1916-
The outlaw breed
```

Printed and bound in Great Britain by
Bookcraft, Midsomer Norton, Somerset

THE OUTLAW BREED

Chapter One

UNDENIABLY, THAT YEARLING had a lot of spirit. It jerked and flopped wildly at the end of the rope, blatting its frenzy, while the man in the roan's saddle grinned and played it like a trout on a fishline. The other pair of riders seemed to be doing nothing much except sit quietly and enjoy the contest.

Jesse Craven saw it all from the fringe of the cedars, where he had pulled rein, and his eyes were pinched and murky with anger. That was a Broad R steer, and this was Broad R grass, where such riders had no right to be. A couple were strangers who bore the plain mark of the range tramp—patched and shapeless clothing, worn rigs, horses as scrubby as themselves. But the third one, the big, yellow-haired man on the sorrel, was Dade Haggis; and it was the sight of Dade that made Jesse's back hairs bristle.

His lean, dark jaw set hard as he spurred the buckskin. They didn't see him right away. The other saddletramp had lit down now and was moving in on the struggling steer. A grab at a leg, a deft twist, sent it flopping; at once the man had a knee on the heaving red side, and a skinning knife's blade glinted in his hand. The yearling made a last effort to escape and then fell still—its eyes rolled back, the red tongue lolling, the soft throat stretched for the blade to slit.

That was when the man on the roan looked up and,

seeing Jesse, gave warning. The one with the knife jerked around, whipping stringy hair that had fallen to bracket a long, bony face. Dade Haggis showed no expression at all as the newcomer reined in, but his cold eyes looked dangerous.

There was danger in Jesse, too. While the buckskin stomped restively under him, he told the man with the knife, "Let him up."

Still kneeling in the long, cured grass, the range tramp gave him a hostile look. "Go off and die!"

All three were armed, with six-guns in holsters or shoved behind their belts. Dade Haggis also carried a saddle carbine under his right knee. But Jesse, with a rope-scarred hand resting on his own cedar-handled Colt, had the advantage; the trio only stared at him, and when nobody moved he told the one in the grass, "I'll take no foolishness. Throw the knife away and slip that rope off him."

The man had no real choice. Shrugging elaborately, he flipped his knife into the dirt and straightened, slapping at his jeans. A jerk of the rope set the steer free; it scrambled to its feet and went bawling away. And while the rider of the roan began pulling his line in and coiling it, the second range tramp turned his back on Jesse and moved stiff-legged toward his waiting horse.

Jesse Craven turned his pinched look on Dade Haggis. "I don't know your friends, Dade," he said flatly. "Introduce me." Dade only glared, not answering him. The other man had found his stirrup and he lifted himself into a shabby saddle and gave the ugly knothead a jerk of the reins. His partner on the roan had his rope coiled and hung across the pommel, and he too had started his horse sidling away.

The gun slid out of Jesse's holster, falling level on the three of them. "I said, I want some names!"

That stopped the furtive movements. There was an exchange of looks. Finally, with another shrug, the one who had just remounted answered gruffly, "Arch Suttle."

"Pete Horn," said the man on the roan, as Jesse's glance slid sharply toward him. Jesse nodded.

"That's better!" he grunted. "All right, Arch Suttle and Pete Horn. You just take your no-good hides off Broad R grass, and don't let me set eyes on either of you again. As for you, Dade—" he swung on the yellow-haired man, who hadn't made any move or altered his half-amused expression—"you watch it! You and the riffraff you run with are going to push me too far one of these days."

The tramp whose name was Arch Suttle let a sneer touch his unshaven lips. "You know this pilgrim, Haggis?" he demanded boldly, keeping a red stare on Jesse. "Who the hell is he? He talks big."

Dade answered, "Why, this is my cousin I told you about. Broad R's high an' mighty ramrod."

"Second cousin, Dade," Jesse shot at him. "Don't make it any closer than it is."

"Oh?" Dade Haggis gave him a knowing, cryptic grin. "You might be a little surprised to know just how close!"

Whatever that was supposed to mean, Jesse Craven could make nothing out of it. He frowned and let it go, saying angrily, "You're doing more than anyone, Dade, to give our people a bad name with folks down here on Buel Creek. I'm telling you now to stop it, or I may have to! Now, take your saddletramp friends and get out of here. Move!"

He saw them pass a look around. Afterward, apparently unready to make an issue of it, they all turned their horses. At a slow walk they rode away from him up the long rise, cured grass stirring and whispering around the hoofs of their mounts.

Jesse was surprised; he hadn't thought they would give in so easily. When they had gone some thirty yards, he holstered his gun. The skinning knife lay where it had been tossed, its blade reflecting a smear of sunlight. He lifted the reins to ride on, then at a second thought turned back and stepped down to get the knife.

He was just stooping for it when hoofbeats started a sudden drumming, and he looked up to catch a glimpse of a horse barreling straight down on him.

Jesse plunged frantically backward, a fraction too slow —the horses's muscled shoulder struck and sent him staggering. Somehow he got his balance, and as ground and trees and sky stopped their reeling he saw that the rider had spun his horse again, in the slick grass, and was coming at him a second time. Jesse saw Arch Suttle's ugly face grinning as the man swung and drove his knotheaded mount straight at him; yonder, where they had hauled rein, the other pair was yelling their man on.

In the effort to give ground Jesse's boot slipped and he thought he was going right under those lumbering hoofs.

At the last minute he caught himself and swerved away. The ground trembled; the big shape thundered past within inches. And, twisting to make a quick grab, Jesse managed to hook his fingers around the instep of the rider's boot in passing; he gave the foot a solid yank.

His arm felt as though it would be wrenched from the socket, but he held on. The boot left its stirrup. The horse ran right out from under its rider, and Arch Suttle hit the ground solidly on face and belly, with arms and legs flung wide. Jesse already had his gun out and he turned, panting, to see about the other pair; but now, as they saw how this little joke had ended, their shouting had died and the jeering grins had faded. Nobody touched a gun.

Suttle, the wind knocked out of him, was retching and sobbing for breath. Jesse nudged him with a boot toe. "Up!" he grunted, harshly. It took a couple of kicks but he got the man on his feet, doubled over and staggering and hugging his belly. Jesse was so blazing furious that the prod of his gun barrel dug deep into the prisoner's spine. "Now, get going!" he ordered, tightly. "Before I knock your head in!"

Pete Horn had caught the flying reins as the riderless horse tried to swerve past. He held it now and Suttle, groaning at every limping step, went hobbling across the grass and on the second try managed to pull himself somehow into the saddle. When he was up he huddled over the horn, looking white and sick. He had lost his hat and didn't appear even to miss it.

They rode away in a dead silence, without any threats this time. But Jesse waited until all three were out of sight before slipping his gun back into holster. He was drenched with sweat; when he ran a sleeve across his face his arm trembled. That had been too damned close!

The fury boiling in him settled on his cousin Dade. He said aloud, "I'm damned if I ain't gonna have to cut him down to size, one of these days!" He'd done it before on occasion, when they were boys growing up together on the scrub timber bench above the basin. There'd always been that mutual dislike; and though it was years since the last of those bare-knuckled mixups—and Dade Haggis in maturity had filled out some ten or fifteen tough pounds heavier than his younger cousin—Jesse was not afraid of tackling him any time that called for it.

If Dade kept this sort of thing up, the time might be soon. A man could feel tension growing in the atmosphere, in the same way he could feel the dry charge of electricity that a storm built up in advance of its coming. The storm threatening Buel Creek country was like that. It had been growing from small things, but now the clouds were of proportions to sober a fellow like Jesse Craven and turn him edgy. Jesse knew he would be at its center whenever the storm did break loose.

Trouble started, often enough, with talk, and so it had been during this dry summer. Now that it was August, even Jesse Craven could no longer close his eyes or his ears to it. He knew that Lorn Mathison, for one, was doing more than letting off steam when he claimed his Spade Bit was losing slow dribbles of its fine blooded stock, and that the people up on the benches—Jesse's people—probably were taking them. And now Jesse had the evidence of his own eyes to suggest that such claims might have some truth to them—truth about Dade Haggis, anyway, even if not of Jesse's father and brothers. Yet if things came to real trouble, the Cravens would be tarred with the same brush. Folks didn't make distinctions among the various families living on the bench.

As he mounted and put his buckskin into its slow, rolling lope toward Broad R headquarters, Jesse's troubled thoughts came back again to Lorn Mathison. That was because of the scene he'd had with the Spade Bit owner, earlier today—a scene which served warning that Mathison was nearly at the end of his patience.

"If you're going up on the bench soon, you can carry a message for me, Craven," he'd said.

"I don't often run errands."

Jesse had known he shouldn't have talked that bluntly, but Mathison's arrogance always brought out the uncurried side of him. It had even pleased him to see the angry sting of color his words brought to the rancher's hollowed cheeks.

"You'll run this errand! You'll tell that old man of yours his damned scrub bull broke down the wire and got into my breeding pasture last night. No knowing how long he was in there. We had a hell of a time chasing him out. You tell old Bob Craven to keep his bull penned, if he ever wants to see him again."

"I'll tell him," Jesse had said. "But don't ever let me

catch you using a gun on that bull! You understand?"

He'd watched a muscle leap in Mathison's grooved cheek. "Why, damn it, I've got thousands of dollars tied up in blooded stock; I'll not have mongrel stuff from the benches getting into it and ruining my calf drop! What's more, I'm warning you now that if those Cravens and Haggises and the rest of them don't leave my beef alone, their cheap cattle may not be the only scrubs that Spade Bit will have orders to use bullets on!"

That was all they had said, but in light of this encounter with Dade Haggis it had been enough.

An hour later Jesse was still tramping his treadmill of futile and inconclusive worry as he stood before a mirror in the empty bunkhouse, and used a long-shanked razor to mow down the day's crop of beard. When he nicked himself he swore and flicked bloody lather through the open window; but it really wasn't the bluntness of the blade that irritated him, or the stubbornness of his beard. He scarcely saw the scowling face in the mirror, with its lean planes, or the eyes that squinted in concentration over the job his big, rope-burned hands were doing with the razor.

The eyes narrowed suddenly, and the razor paused in midstroke. Something seemed to be missing—the steady, slow creaking of the swing, over on the veranda of the main house. Ever since he started cleaning up, that sound had been a part of his consciousness. He had known that if he looked through the open door of the bunkhouse he would see the woman's dim figure seated in the swing, her bare arms gleaming in the shadow. But now that monotonous rhythm had stopped, and in its place was the Saturday-afternoon silence of an almost deserted ranch.

Wind washed like surf through a row of poplars that made a slim and stately line across the meadow, their trunks shadowed by the bare ridge behind the ranch yard, their golden heads swaying against a deep August sky. In the kitchen shack the old cook was banging about, and singing roundup songs in a voice that suggested he had been at the vanilla extract again. There were just these three left from the weekly exodus to Bueltown: himself, and the battered cook, and George Rickart's handsome wife.

Jesse shrugged, and made the finishing strokes that

whipped the last of the lather from his dark cheeks. He wiped the razor blade, folded it into the handle and laid it on the shelf. He dipped his face into the basin and dried it on a towel draped about his shoulders, afterwards tossing the towel aside. He picked up the tin washbowl, meaning to empty it—and went suddenly motionless as he saw Blanche Rickart standing in the doorway.

He had no idea how long she might have been there, her shoulders against the edge of the open door and her arms folded beneath her full breasts. She wore a full skirt, a sleeveless apple-green blouse of silk that set off the beauty of her piled-up, silver-blonde hair. No woman, not even Blanche, ever invaded the male world of a bunkhouse, and for a moment he could only stare, before he found his tongue. "Something you wanted?"

She shook her head, a lazy gesture. "Just to talk." Her glance rested on his scowling face, moved to the slabby muscle that plated his bare chest and shoulders. Faintly embarrassed, Jesse turned and set down the basin of soapy water he had been holding, and then took up the clean shirt off his bunk.

He slipped into it and was working with the buttons as Blanche pushed away from the door, with an easy, sinuous movement, and walked toward him.

It was a long, low-ceilinged room, nearly unfurnished except for the bunks that lined the walls, a pot-bellied stove standing in a box of cinders, a scarred table and chairs. Everywhere was the careless litter of the men who lived in it. Blanche came as far as the table, and placed the fingertips of one slim, white hand upon it. She looked at the shirt Jesse was tucking behind his waistband and she asked, "Going to town?"

"Among other places." He felt an impulse to add, "Why don't you ever try it? Might do you good to get out among people, instead of sitting here all the time." But it was not his place to suggest it. Jesse was well aware of the contempt in which she held this country and its people—everything that was so far removed from the life she'd been accustomed to before marrying George Rickart.

She looked around the bunkroom. Washed into its corners was a forgotten jetsam of coverless magazines, of empty bottles and discarded clothing and gear. Cards and poker chips littered the spur-scarred table top. She picked up a blue chip, then tossed it from her with a shudder of disgust for its grimy, greasy feel. "A pigsty!" she exclaimed. "How can men live like this?"

"We get used to it."

The words brought him her scornful glance. "I'd be ashamed to admit it!"

Jesse swallowed a quick resentment. He went on buttoning his shirt, watching Blanche Rickart and waiting, puzzled, for her to say whatever she had to say to him. As always, he felt acutely uncomfortable in the presence of this blonde woman who was so totally different from any kind that he had ever known.

She must have sensed how he felt. She came closer, looking at him with her head on one side and a faint smile tugging at her red mouth. "What's the matter, Jesse? You don't like me, do you?"

"I hope I never said or done anything to—"

"Oh, come now! You've hardly been civil!"

He frowned, shaking his head. He assuredly didn't want any misunderstanding between himself and his boss's wife; actually he had paid her little attention since the day George Rickart had brought her back from Denver. Perhaps he felt a stirring of attraction, but he had no intention of letting it go any further than that. And if she seemed to him oddly suited for a man as bloodless as Rickart, that was not his concern.

He said now, "If I've offended you, it wasn't intentional: I've got so much on my mind I suppose I don't notice other people."

"I'm sure that's it," she agreed quickly, and now her smile took on a sudden warmth. She even placed a hand on Jesse's arm, in an intimacy that made him aware of the heat that began to spread across the back of his neck.

"You're forgiven," she told him, lightly. "I know how hard you've worked. I've been watching you, these two years since I came here. I've seen you go from top-hand to foreman—and now, a full partnership! That's a record to be proud of."

He nodded. "It's kind of you, Mrs. Rickart."

"Mrs. Rickart? From the man who's soon to be my husband's partner?" She took her hand away, shaking her head at him, still smiling. "My name is Blanche, Jesse!"

He didn't answer.

"You want to finish dressing," she said, and Jesse stood and watched her walk without hurry to the door. But there she swung around and faced him again, and now she was not smiling. George Rickart's diamond, on the ring finger of her left hand, flashed as she stroked the flesh of her bare right arm. "Were you planning to go anywhere else, this afternoon?" she asked. "Besides town?"

"I may be." He said it carefully, knowing what was to follow.

"Up on the bench, I suppose?" Blanche's mouth curled down, and seeing the answer in his eyes she added, "I thought as much!"

Jesse felt a stir of inward anger. "Any reason I shouldn't? That's the place where I came from. My folks are still there. My father's having a birthday. I'm expected."

"I didn't mean to make you angry," George Rickart's wife said quickly. "I know this is none of my business. But aside from what Lorn Mathison and a few others are saying about those people, I'm thinking of you, Jesse—the partnership, and your place in the valley. You've come far since you left the bench. Don't spoil it now. Don't let them drag you back to their level and their kind of life. You've got fine things in you; but that's in your blood, too, and your background. For your own good, you must never stop fighting it."

He heard her out, in a kind of haze of anger and astonishment at her frankness. When Blanche was finished he merely stood and looked at her for a long moment; then he shook his head, and his craggy face was hard set, his eyes cold.

"I'm not ashamed of what I am," he told her, bluntly. "Maybe the bench folks ain't long on schooling. Maybe they're not much for hard work, and for pushing ahead. Could be even that they fight and drink more than they should. Just the same, they could teach some I know a few things about getting fun out of life. And anyway, they're my people. I won't stand by and listen to anybody run 'em down!"

It was more than he had intended to say; he clamped his jaw, expecting Blanche to lash back at him. Dismally, he knew the last thing he could afford just now was to get in bad with this woman whose dislike, if he roused it, could go far to destroying the planned partnership with George Rickart. He regretted intensely letting the words be jolted out of him.

But Blanche only looked at him, the expression of her

spoiled, handsome face unreadable. All she said was, "Very well, Jesse. Let's forget it." She turned and walked out.

Jesse stood and looked after her for a long time, frowning and troubled.

Chapter Two

BUELTOWN WAS NOT MUCH. There were three blocks of business houses, including four saloons and a miscellany of wooden-fronted stores. There were a few fair-sized homes belonging to the better merchants, and then a fringe of shacks and sheds and board fences and privies, mostly needing paint. The old covered bridge that crossed the creek, on the main freight road out of the valley, had a slight list to one side and its loose planks raised a rumbling thunder whenever a wagon and team went through.

But this was the only town Jesse Craven had ever seen, and it looked good enough to him. On a flat to the north, that was hard-packed and worn clean of grass, stood the one-room school with its iron bell. Jesse had learned his reading and writing and figuring there, and a bit of history and geography. He'd ridden a mule down from the bench country every day, braving the hostility of the town kids on the one hand, and the joshing of his bench neighbors and relatives on the other. Of all the Cravens, he alone had seen any sense in rising at three in the morning to buck the winter drifts, just for the foolishness of book learning. . . .

Dust lay thick and loose in the unpaved streets, where the stomping hoofs of tired horses had pounded it along the tie poles. The hitch racks were well lined this Saturday afternoon, especially the ones in front of Bueltown's saloons. There was a steady traffic through the streets, and the thud of hoofs and squeal of axles beat against the high false fronts. Ranch wagons, loaded with a week's supplies waited to take the homeward haul.

Jesse's business was quickly taken care of. The hitching post in front of the Colorado Bar being crowded, he tied across the street and ducked through the traffic, elbowing open the swinging doors. At once he was hit by the familiar smells of men and whisky and horses, and heard the familiar sounds. A poker game was going at one of the card tables, and the bar had a lineup. Tom Nealy, one of the Broad R cowboys, yelled a greeting and made room for him as Jesse rang his spurs through the litter of floor sawdust.

He hooked a heel upon the bar rail, put both elbows on the wood and catching the bartender's eye called for rye whisky—the best. It passed muster and he ordered a sealed bottle to take along. The barkeep put it in a paper sack for him.

Then Tom Nealy offered to buy the drinks and afterward Jesse stood Tom for a round. It was a week since he'd had any liquor and it warmed him, helped to lay some of the irritation that was still working in him after the events of this afternoon. Feeling better, he refused another drink and walked outside again, carrying his purchase. He paused for a moment on the veranda, but could think of nothing more that needed doing. So he went back across the street to where his horse was tied, in front of the milliner's.

A shiny black buggy had just pulled in and Jesse nodded a greeting to the man who was tying at the rack. Dave Clevenger said, "Afternoon, Jesse." He was a rather small, graying man, habitually worried about business and his ranch, but one whose fairmindedness Jesse Craven respected and liked. He looked at the obvious shape of the package in Jesse's hand and lifted an eyebrow. "Can you put all that away by yourself?"

"It's sort of a birthday present."

"Oh, yes—your father's." Clevenger's mouth quirked humorously. "But I always heard the Cravens cooked their own."

"And only a Craven can drink it," Jesse assured him. "This is for a special occasion."

"Well, give old Bob my regards," Dave said, and Jesse promised to. He opened a pocket of his saddlebag and stowed the quart bottle away, and then turned as Dave Clevenger helped his daughter out of the buggy.

Jesse should have done that chore himself, but always in the presence of Catherine Clevenger he was nearly tongue-tied; and to this was added the discomfort of having let her see him with a quart of whisky in his hand. So he only touched his hatbrim, and received Catherine's cool, unsmiling nod in return.

Catherine had been one of the kids who had teased him the most, when he used to ride the mule down from the bench to school. Through the years Jesse had watched her grow from a leggy tomboy with a wild shock of raven-black hair, to the aloof, slim-hipped beauty who walked away from him now, a hand on her father's arm. Never in all this time had Jesse been able to make friends with her. Never had he conquered a crippling shyness that somehow quelled and cowed him when in this girl's superior presence. As he stood there by his buckskin's shoulder and looked after the two of them—Catherine a little taller than her father, graceful and very sure of herself—he ruefully wondered if he would ever find the courage to treat her as an equal.

Not that she was a snob; no daughter of Dave Clevenger's could ever be that. There was something else, something buried behind her aloof reserve toward Jesse Craven that he simply could not fathom, try as he would . . .

"Craven!"

The voice snapped his head around quickly. Jesse hadn't noticed the horseman moving toward him. This was a man in a high-cantled saddle, a well-built figure in a black hat and black shirt and trousers—a drooping-eyed man who held the reins negligently in the tapering fingers of his left hand, while his right hung free near the silver-mounted gun in the holster that snugged his hip. He looked down at Jesse, with a look that held something contemptuous in it.

He said, "I got a word for you, Craven. A message from my boss."

"If it's about the bull," Jesse answered shortly, "I've already heard. I saw Mathison a little earlier. He told me himself."

Roy Shull regarded him for a moment in silence. "That's good," he said then. "That's fine! You look like a pretty smart boy, Craven. I don't suppose you have to be told more than once. Now, do you?" And when Jesse didn't answer: "You just better see that the rest of that clan of yours pays as close attention—because if they don't, they're about to lose them a bull."

Jesse stared back, fighting temper. Jesse had never seen Roy Shull's gun skill tested, though the word had drifted in from other ranges. He didn't know how much Lorn Mathison was paying him in wages, though it must run high; but ever since Mathison had brought him to Buel Creek, Jesse had been keenly conscious of the threat that Roy Shull represented.

He was a loaded gun pointed straight at the people that

Mathison hated, for reasons that were not fully clear to Jesse—the families up there on the bench.

Jesse, who was no gunman, tilted his head and looked straight at the gunman and said, harshly, "I'll tell you what I told Mathison! Don't touch that bull—and don't get rough with my folks!"

"Really laying it on the line, ain't you?" Shull murmured, insolently. His eyes, meeting Jesse's hot stare, were cool and mocking. As their looks clashed, a smile twisted the gunman's mouth; he clucked his tongue at his horse, and somehow managed to make the sound a personal insult.

He turned his back then, deliberately, leaving Jesse battling the wish to call a challenge and have it out with him. But it would do no one any good, to go and get himself killed for no purpose. The people on the bench needed him alive! Grim and tight around the mouth, Jesse swung back to his horse and jerked the reins free.

He felt better when he had left the town behind him, and his spirits rose as he took one of the steep trails that led to his folks' place on the bench. Up here, he couldn't hold a bad feeling for long. It was like riding into a different but familiar world, where the burdens a man carried slipped from his shoulders.

Sometime in the past, an upheaval of the earth's crust had raised a fault scarp of raw red rock along a section of the valley's eastern wall. Jammed between the timbered uplands and this drop to rich graze below, the resulting bench had been hard worn by ages of erosion—by the too-rapid runoff of melting snow from the higher hills that had stripped it of its soil and gouged deeply into the face of the scarp itself. Such grass as grew was scant and poor enough; still, it did for the few head of gaunt-ribbed culls that the bench people troubled with. The Cravens and Haggises and Meanses, and the other interlocking families, made do with what they had.

They'd been here for almost thirty years now. From Pike County to begin with, they'd trekked out from Missouri in a general migration to the gold fields when Jesse's dad was a young man. None had found quick wealth. Disappointed, they'd gradually drifted on across the mountains to the western slope, and here taken up squatter rights on this narrow shelf of timber and poor graze that no one else wanted. And this was where Jesse Craven had been born.

Folks down in Bueltown, he supposed, would never understand why he still liked to come back. His folks had nothing, and most of them would never get anywhere; but even if they were ignorant and crude they seemed to breathe a freer air than their anxious and ambitious neighbors in the basin. Right now Jesse was even whistling—something he rarely did since taking on the responsibility of ramrodding George Rickart's Broad R—as he came into sight of his father's place.

It was bare and unattractive. The shake-roofed house and barn and corral had weathered out to a dull gray and they clearly showed the repairs they needed. They crowded back into a timbered hollow, where the rims protected them from the worst of the winter storms. There was an acre in corn and root crops which, together with the beef and game the men brought in and butchered, supplied nearly all the food the family needed. That was the extent of it.

Just now it looked as though Jesse had been almost the last to arrive. Ranch wagons stood about the yard, with teams and saddle horses tied to the wheels. Kids and dogs swarmed busily. Three long trestle tables had been set up, with the women busy putting out food.

Someone caught sight of the newcomer and he rode into a barrage of greetings. His mother came from the kitchen carrying a steaming kettle and glowing with pleasure at sight of him. There was not much display of affection, but even so the pride showed through her casual greeting as she set the kettle down and wiped red, roughened hands on her apron. She was a big woman who had brought three strapping sons and a daughter into the world. Her hair was thinning and turning drab now, but there seemed no lessening of her strength.

All she said was, "We'd given you up. I see you got here in time to eat, anyway."

He grinned at her. "That's how I had it figured, Ma. Where's Ellie? And Bob—I got a present for him."

"Ellie's in the house. You'll find the menfolks out back, seeing to the barbecue. Tell 'em we're ready and waitin' on 'em, whenever they get through fooling around."

"I'll tell 'em."

He hadn't dismounted, and now he sent his horse on around the house, following his nose. The fine smell of roasting meat drifted across the heat and the dust. Now Jesse saw the men, a dozen or more of them, hanging about the barbecue fire where a whole beef turned on a spit, roasting to a beautiful brown. Here were more dogs, and all the male youngsters above the age of eight standing with their hands shoved into hip pockets, carefully imitating every gesture of their elders. The men ranged from Jesse's younger brother Billy to old Rig Means of the wooden leg and the ancient fiddle. Old Rig hadn't yet taken the instrument out of its battered case. It lay on a stump, awaiting its time, while Rig tilted a jug across his elbow and his stringy throat, bristling with white beard stubble, worked to his swallowing.

Lowering the jug of corn, Rig saw Jesse and let out a shout. "Why, here he is now. We been talkin' about you, boy!"

Jesse Craven's partnership in the Broad R was the biggest news the bench had had in a long time. He stepped down from saddle, to be hoorawed and have his back slapped by neighbors and relatives. They'd once laughed at him for trying to better himself, but that wasn't a thing he could hold against them now. They hadn't understood the urge that had driven him. Since it had paid off, they were free enough to admit their mistake without any sign of resentment or jealousy.

Jesse looked around for his dad and found Bob Craven turning the handle of the spit. Jesse walked over, saying, "Hi, Bob." His father nodded. Everyone called him "old Bob" Craven, though he was actually a good deal younger than some of his neighbors. His strong body, in faded overalls and a shirt with its sleeves whacked off, showed few signs of the passing years; his full brown beard was only a little streaked with grey, and his brown eyes were as sharp as ever. He had a powerful beak of a nose, which only Homer, the oldest of the three sons, had inherited. Jesse and young Billy had their looks mostly from their mother.

"Brought you a birthday present," Jesse told him, and turning to his horse he opened the flap of a saddlebag and brought out the whisky. He tossed the bottle to his father.

Bob grinned with pleasure. "Well, what do you think of that!" he cried. "Never tasted this brand in my life, though I got in smellin' distance of it once!" He dug his teeth into the cork, but it was in tight and took considerable worrying and hauling before he dragged it free. "Sixty years old today," he said proudly. "And still got every tooth I was born with!"

Someone told him, "Well, hurry up and take a pull at that bottle and pass it around."

"Yeah," said another. "Spit out the cork, Bob—you won't need it. Bottle will be empty before it gets back to you."

"Don't rush me!" Bob offered the bottle first to Jesse, and when the latter shook his head he put it to his own lips, tilted his head and let the whisky run into his throat. He came up gasping. "Now, that is something like! Jess, if you got nothin' else down at that school, they at least learned you how to pick whisky!" He smacked his lips and passed the bottle on to his nearest neighbor.

"I want to talk with you, Bob," his son told him.

"Sure!" The old man nodded to his youngest boy. "Take charge of the spit, Billy. You burn any part of that meat and I'll roast you!" He threw a heavy arm across Jesse's shoulder then and the two of them walked off toward the horse shed together—two big men, the buckskin trailing behind on its reins.

As Jesse set about stripping saddle and bridle, his father leaned meaty shoulders against a timber and asked, "Everything going all right, son?"

"Right enough." He hauled the heavy stock saddle off and slung it across a rack. He was bringing money from his pocket as he added, "I just thought there might be a few things you or Ma or Ellie could be using—"

Old Bob waved him away. "We're gettin' along. We ain't asking you for money. Wouldn't want you thinkin' so."

"No, take it!" Jesse insisted. "What have I got to spend it on?"

His father gave in, smiling, and shoved the bills deep into a pocket of his overalls. "Much obliged," he said. And, as Jesse turned back to his work: "The partnership deal is really going through, then?"

"Last I heard." Jesse removed the bit from the buckskin's mouth and slipped off the headstall. He gave the horse a clap on the rump and it walked into a stall.

Bob wagged his head. "Well, George Rickart can't be entirely the fool I've always thought he was, then. He at least has the sense to know he can't fill old Ham Rickart's shoes without a spell of help. And he's spotted the one man who'll best run that ranch for him—I'll give him that much credit."

"Ain't the meat about done? Ma said they're waitin' on it."

"Women get too doggoned impatient. It'll be done when I say it is!"

Jesse gave him a careful look. "Incidentally, whose brand happened to be on that yearling? I hope it was a bench animal."

The old man turned on him indignantly. "Of course it was! What are you trying to accuse me of, son?" But then he grinned a little, showing strong white teeth behind the whiskers. "You figure that beef looks a mite fat for this range?"

"I didn't figure anything, Bob. But I think I better warn you—Lorn Mathison is on the prod. That bull of yours has been after his she stuff again. Mathison says next time he'll shoot him!"

The grin faded; old Bob's eyes turned sharp. "He better not try it!"

"Don't be a fool!" Jesse was serious. "He'll do what he says—and he's got Roy Shull to back him if you make trouble. He's not afraid of anybody on this bench. He doesn't like us; he thinks we're a shiftless lot and that our stock endangers the blood strains he's importing. He'd like an excuse to get rid of us."

"I don't aim to take nothin' from him!"

"Never figured you would. Just the same, it wouldn't be smart for you or Homer, or Billy, or one of the others to go throwing a loop over one of those blooded steers, by accident. Don't underestimate him. And for Pete's sake, keep that bull penned!"

Bob frowned, his lower jaw thrust out in a characteristic fashion. "We'll see." Jesse had to be satisfied with that.

He pulled down hay for the buckskin and dumped in a little corn, and then he stood in the door of the shed while he rolled a cigarette and hung it between his lips, and snapped a match to light it with. The noise of the crowd drifted to him. Out by the barbecue fire, a couple of the older boys were having a friendly scrap and Jesse's mouth spread in a grin as he watched them wrestle.

Yonder, Rig Means had his fiddle and was tuning up for the music that would begin after the feed.

Who cared what anyone said? He had sprung from these

people and there was a part of him that couldn't be as well satisfied anywhere else. They were a heavy-handed lot, maybe; they could hate on occasion, but they also knew how to live to the hilt. They knew what really mattered. With all their poverty, they were nonetheless free of the galling frictions of that practical world of the valley—the petty greeds, the worry about market prices and getting ahead of your neighbor.

If they liked you they'd give you an arm. If they didn't like you—well, that was something else again.

Chapter Three

DINNER WAS ABOUT READY. Old Bob and his boys came toting big washtubs piled with steaming cuts from the barbecue. One of the dogs had got hold of a bone and the whole pack went tearing across the yard, snarling and yapping; Bob Craven booted them out of the way, shouting, "All right, folks! Come on. Let's tear into this while it's fit to eat!" The crowd began to collect around the long tables that seemed to groan under their burden of food.

As Jesse came around the house, he nearly collided with Dade Haggis, who was swinging off his roach-maned sorrel. Jesse hadn't seen his cousin ride up; he halted and shot a quick look around as his cousin met him with a narrow, mean-eyed expression.

"Lookin' for somebody?" Dade asked heavily.

"Yes—your friends. I'm glad to see you didn't bring 'em. Saves me the chore of booting them off the place."

"Think you could?" Dade added, his shoulders settling. "You figure maybe to boot me off?"

Jesse eyed his cousin, measuring his own raw length of bone and muscle against his size. "If I have to. Mind your manners, though, and you can stay."

His cousin's mouth twisted. "Golly, thanks!" he jeered, and laughed coarsely. It was all Jesse could do to keep from hitting him. He settled for a contemptuous look, and then shouldered past Dade and walked on to join the crowd around the tables.

Jesse's sister Ellie came from the house, carrying two hot loaves of bread wrapped in dishtowels. She had a strangely abstracted look about her. Jesse waited, but she went by without appearing to notice him. Puzzled, he called after her, "Hey, carrot top! What's the matter with you?"

That name usually got a rise out of her, because her hair was scarcely red at all—hardly more so than Jesse's own brown mane that showed a coppery tinge in certain lights. But she didn't rise to the bait this time. Even though he was her favorite brother, and it was over two weeks since his last visit, Ellie only turned to say lifelessly, across a shoulder, "Oh—hello, Jesse."

He stood and stared after her. This was so unlike Ellie that for a moment he couldn't believe it. Her small heart-shaped face was pale, and she seemed wholly dispirited. If there hadn't been such a crowd he would have gone after her and demanded an explanation; but he supposed that when a girl reached her age she probably had her moody times that had to be fought through by herself. He could remember how it had been with him, at seventeen.

Later, he would find a better chance to talk to her and make her tell him what was wrong. Now, trying not to worry about her, he turned to mix with the crowd that was going after the food in raucous friendliness. One of his aunts shoved a china mug of coffee into his hand and told him to pitch in if he wanted anything to eat. Somebody else dumped a chunk of steaming beef on his plate. Yonder, Bob was being hoorawed over the size of the mountain of food he was piling up for himself.

Blanche Rickart, like enough, would have thought it all loud and coarse; but it was an atmosphere in which each person was accepted on his own valuation. They showed that they were glad to have you here, and that you belonged. It was a feeling he'd never known down on Buel Creek, where a man reserved something from his neighbor, not wanting to be unarmed by too much frankness and risk being left behind in the race to stay ahead of the rest.

He found his mother standing next to him and he laid an arm across her shoulders. "Food smells right good, Ma."

She smiled up at him, but her eyes were serious as they moved across his face. "Everything going all right with you, son?" she asked him.

"Why, sure. Right as rain." But the serious look in her eyes didn't alter.

"I see more changes in you every time you come. I'm just

worried that you ain't happy in that job. It's a big one."

"Now don't worry about me any," he assured her, but he wondered if the assurance was as convincing as he tried to make it. "What could make you think anything's wrong?"

Maud Craven didn't answer his question, for at that moment there was a crash of broken crockery. It went unnoticed in the general hubbub around the tables, but Jesse and his mother happened to be facing the house and, looking that way, they saw what had happened. Ellie stood in the kitchen doorway, a broken bowl of greens at her feet; she leaned against the jamb and stared at it, motionless, with both hands pressed against her thin cheeks. They saw her sway slightly.

Jesse blurted, "Ma! Is Ellie sick?"

His mother laid down her serving spoon. Jesse saw the sternness that had at once come into her face; without a word she turned and started for the house. Puzzled and alarmed, Jesse stood where he was and watched his mother go to Ellie, speak to her, and then put an arm around her daughter and lead her inside. No one else appeared to notice.

Suddenly Jesse put down his food and started for the house himself.

The kitchen was a steaming clutter of cookery, and empty when he stepped inside. He crossed to the door of Ellie's room, which opened off it. Within he could hear a broken murmur of voices; his knock went unanswered. For just a moment he hesitated, and then deliberately he pushed the door open and walked in.

They were on the bed, Ellie huddled in her mother's arms. His mother shook her head at Jesse, but he came in anyway and closed the door behind him. He looked down at the pair of them. "What's wrong?" he demanded.

"Nothing," his mother answered, shortly. Ellie, weeping, had her face buried in her mother's ample bosom. Then, in savage bitterness, the older woman blurted, "That Dade!"

"Dade?" Understanding flooded Jesse, and unbelief, and then a fury that shook him. He lifted his big hand, ready in that moment to strike this sister that he loved more than any other being. "Ellie, you ain't gone and shamed yourself—"

His mother broke in, her voice leaden and tired-sounding. "Let her alone, Jess. Blame me, if anybody. I never dreamed—She's so young, and I never thought of that skunk Dade Haggis coming around, sweet-talking her."

Slowly, Jesse dropped his arm. It was trembling. He stared at the two of them. He turned and looked blindly through the window, at pine turned golden and green in the slanting light of late afternoon, and a bare rocky peak lifting above the timber.

"Don't suppose there could be any mistake?"

"No mistake, I reckon," his mother said.

Jesse looked at his sister. "Have you told Dade?" The coppery hair stirred as she nodded, face buried against her mother's apron. "What did he say?"

"Didn't say nothin'." Ellie's voice was muffled. "He—laughed at me!"

The muscles of Jesse's face were like a stiff mask. "I'll kill him," he said then in a low, tight voice. His mother shook her head.

"What good would that do? Either for her or the baby?"

Jesse said, with revulsion, "But surely she doesn't want to marry him? She couldn't love a skunk like that!"

"How do you know what she feels or wants?" his mother lashed out at him. "Of course she loves him. Do you think there'd be any other reason—"

"All right," he cut in, shortly. And he heeled around and walked out of the room, not answering when his mother called after him in quick alarm. . . .

They didn't seem to have been missed. The eating was in full swing; laughter and talk rose loudly from the people clustered around the long tables, or moving about with plates and cups in their hands. As Jesse came out of the house someone called to him, but he didn't even hear.

He had made his quick survey and already located Dade Haggis, sitting off by himself on a grounded wagon tongue. Jesse walked straight toward him. Dade had made himself a sandwich of bread and beef, and was holding this in one hand and a tin coffee cup in the other. He had just taken a big bite when he saw Jesse and he went motionless, one cheek pouched. Jesse saw his eyes narrow, and from Dade's whole manner could tell that his cousin knew exactly what he had learned and what he wanted.

Slowly, Dade straightened and put both boots on the ground as Jesse came to a stand, facing him. Jesse's hands were working at his sides and he could feel the tightness throughout his body.

"Well?" he said, harshly.

"You heard about it, then?" grunted Dade, around the mouthful of bread and meat.

"I heard."

The other shrugged, loosely. "Big brother, huh?" He looked down into his cup, rotating it. "Just forget it, boy. You're wasting your time." He tossed his head back and drank.

"You're gonna marry her, Dade."

The tawny eyes flashed at him across the rim of the cup. "Like hell!"

"I mean it!" Jesse said, his voice quiet with a suppressed fury. "You can't get my sister in trouble and then not do anything!"

Deliberately, Dade Haggis finished drinking. He shook the dregs from his cup and tossed it into the grass. He threw the rest of his sandwich after it, and came to his feet.

"You listen to me," he said tightly, harshly. "This is twice today you've tried to ride me, and I ain't takin' it. You understand?" His mouth twisted in a sneer. "What's the fuss, anyway? What's one bastard kid more or less?"

Jesse wiped the sneer back against his teeth, with the unwarned swing of a hard fist.

Dade went off balance and stumbled against the tongue of the wagon and fell sideward, to hands and knees. For a moment Jesse stood and looked at him, feeling the tingling of his fist. He saw Dade shake his head; then his cousin spat out the food he had been chewing on, and there was blood mixed in it. Dade reared up, reaching a hand to the wagon tongue to lever himself to his feet.

The hair had fallen in long yellow wings at either side of his face. He wiped a wrist across his bleeding mouth. Suddenly, with an animal sound in his throat, he lunged at Jesse.

The latter faded back before his rush, meeting it with a forearm raised to block the wild fist Dade threw. He struck Dade in the ribs and the other man staggered, and Jesse told him hoarsely, "If you want a whipping, Dade, I'll sure give you one! You got it coming!"

Dade cursed and charged him again, and Jesse had to give ground. Dimly he sensed that the whole yardful of people were swarming around now, yelling and excited at the outbreak of a fight. They didn't know what the trouble was, but that didn't make any difference. He heard his brother Homer shouting from just behind him, "Go to it, Jesse! Tear him open!"

The shouting and the crowding had no effect on him at all. He went after that bruised and sneering face. He smashed it with his fists, getting a release in the pain of his hands when they struck solid flesh and bone. He scarcely felt the blows Dade gave him. He kept boring right in, hardly even thinking to keep a guard.

He saw Dade's hated face turn bloody. He felt a slimy wetness flow blindingly into his own right eye and realized vaguely that it was blood, that the eye was hurt and swelling shut. Nothing could stop him. Dade Haggis's face had turned slack-lipped; Dade was tiring, panting through his mouth and dribbling blood and slobber. There was a look of fear in Dade's eyes.

Then suddenly Dade was off his feet, down in the dirt. Through the drift of dust they had kicked up, Jesse saw him rolling away with arms clamped about his head, expecting the kick of his enemy's boot. Jesse let him go. He stood panting, bringing his wind under control while he waited for Dade to get his feet under him. Instead, sensing that the kick wasn't coming, Dade pulled himself slowly to his knees, and stopped there.

He glared at Jesse, hair plastered in the mud and blood and sweat that smeared his face. He ran a sleeve across his eyes; his mouth twisted and he shot a look about him at the ring of watching faces.

And then Dade was on his feet, and almost too late Jesse saw the shine of the knife in his hand. He managed to twist aside, and felt the tug of the blade as it ripped through his shirt and laid heat along his ribs. With a quick grab he tried to capture Dade's wrist, and failed. He stumbled, attempting to get away from the knife when it lashed at him again. Triumph was a wicked gleam in the other man's eyes. Dade lunged again and the knife swooped; its point clicked against the buckle of Jesse's belt—it had missed ripping him by that narrow margin.

He made another desperate grab, and this time his hand closed on Dade's wrist. The wrist and his own palm were sweaty, slippery; in the fraction of an instant before Dade could wrench free, Jesse pivoted and brought the arm, elbow locked, across his hip. He bore down, trying to make Dade drop the knife. Dade struggled to get away; his left fist struck wildly and landed just under Jesse's straining heart, and almost made him black out.

Then, with his free hand, Jesse reached and caught Dade just under the chin; his fingers spread over the other's bloody cheeks and mouth and eyes. Grimly he put on the pressure. Dade would not break. They strained like that, toe to toe, until Jesse felt the muscles of his arms begin to tremble, and Dade's other hand pawing him for a hold.

Suddenly Dade's feet went out from under him, and he pivoted on the arm trapped across Jesse's hip. He struck the ground hard on his back—so hard that he bounced. And Jesse hurled himself upon him.

A single twist loosened Dade's fingers and shook the knife free; a belt across the jaw took most of the remaining fight out of him. but Jesse was too angry then to quit. He straddled his cousin and hit him again and again—punishing blows that rocked his head from side to side.

"Enough!" The tortured groan broke from Dade's torn mouth. Somehow it jarred home and Jesse stopped the next blow in mid-swing. He looked at his enemy's face, and at his bleeding knuckles. He was panting with exertion. He opened and closed his hand, and was numbly pleased to find that it worked. Then aware again of other people, he lifted his head and looked around him, his lips slack and swollen. His mouth was dry. He swallowed, and touched his tongue to his lips and found that they hurt.

"You need any more convincing?" he demanded hoarsely. "Or are you satisfied that it's time you got married and settled down?"

The beaten man's eyes were only half open; they were looking at Jesse, hating him. Jesse said, again, "Are you?" and lifted his fist.

Dade stammered, thickly, "You don't have to hit me again!"

"All right. The circuit rider will be through again in another two or three weeks. Just remember, you got a date with him. If you ain't around for it, I'll go wherever you are and drag you back."

Weakly, Dade Haggis managed to nod agreement. "Get off, will you?" he moaned. "You're killin' me."

Jesse dragged himself to his feet. His knees were trembling. Dade flopped over and tried to rise, but collapsed on his face. Jesse stood looking down at him; then he picked up the knife. He walked over to a wagon and shoved the blade deep into a crack between two timbers, and gave a quick thrust that snapped the blade off clean. He threw the knife handle from him.

The scene blew up, then, in a babble of talk. One or two came to look at the man lying beaten in the dirt. His brother Homer stared at Jesse's battered face and demanded, "What brought that on, Jess? For the love of Pete—"

"Ma'll tell you." Jesse got his hat that he'd lost early in the fight, and beating it against his knee he started straight across the yard to the horse shed. Homer called after him, "Where you goin'?"

"To get my bronc," he muttered harshly.

His mother stood in the kitchen door, pale of face, her hands knotted tight in the folds of her apron. Jesse veered and went to her. He said, "Tell Ellie it's all settled. He'll marry her."

She cried anxiously, "Don't go, Jesse. You're hurt! And you never even ate anything."

"I'll be all right," he answered. "I ain't hungry."

He went on, bloody face grim and eyes set straight ahead. The crowd watched him. He was tired and dispirited; Dade had been a tough opponent. His face, his bruised fists, and that knife scratch across his ribs were hurting him.

But the worst hurt of all was inside. Little Ellie! She was a good girl; she'd been raised properly and she knew right and wrong—whatever remarks some bluenoses in Bueltown might have to make about the bench people's morals were they to hear of this! Those folks didn't have skunks like Dade Haggis to reckon with.

Right now all Jesse wanted was to get clear away from there. He piled the gear on his horse and swung painfully astride. The first gray of twilight was already staining the chilling air as he rode out, not looking at anyone.

Chapter Four

AFTER WEEKS OF DRY WEATHER a real rain had come up, with the creeks running chocolate-colored and tearing down their banks. Within forty minutes the clouds had broken, but they still dotted the pale sky and ran their flowing shadows across a freshened range. The air had a cooler touch to it—as though this brief storm had been the first break of the summer's hold, the first early presage of autumn.

So it was that when someone ran off a jag of Lorn Mathison's blooded beef stock, there could be no question that the cattle had only drifted. The prints were plain in the softened ground, and they told the story: three riders who knew precisely what they wanted, and went about their work with a practiced efficiency.

Jesse learned first about the trouble when he rode into Broad R headquarters that morning, having just made a check on a vega of winter feed where stock had broken down the wire. At a little distance he saw a trio of horsemen riding away, and judged that two of these were Mathison and Roy Shull, his shadow; the third looked like Dave Clevenger. They were out of sight by the time he reached the yard and reined over by the corral; but as he started to swing down, Tom Nealy came to him with the news. Jesse could tell it was trouble before the puncher spilled it out. His face went bleak as he listened.

"How many head?" he demanded, interrupting.

"Twenty, Mathison says, from one of his best holdings. And three men driving 'em off, headed for the benches. He went and picked up Dave Clevenger for a witness. He says he figures—well—"

"No need to tell me! He's got it in for the Cravens because of that fool bull. He'd give a lot to pin something on them!" Eyes darkened by his thoughts, Jesse turned back to his horse. The buckskin was not too jaded; deliberately he jerked the cinch tighter.

Nealy asked him, anxiously, "What are you going to do, Jesse?"

"I ain't sure," he answered, and swung again to the saddle.

Three riders! If that damned Dade—

He heard his name being called and, recognizing George Rickart's voice, swung about. Rickart was standing at the edge of the porch; he sent the buckskin over there.

His boss came down a step into the sunlight, and from the look of his face Jesse knew at once he was in for something disagreeable. The feeling became even stronger when, drawing nearer, he caught sight of Blanche standing on the porch, behind her husband.

He halted, thumbing the Stetson back from his forehead, and Rickart said, bluntly, "Nealy told you?"

Jesse nodded.

George Rickart had an air of softness about him that gave the impression of a man gone a little past his prime, although he was only forty. Too many of his best years had been wasted in the role of a rich man's son waiting for his father to die. Now that the big Broad R was at last his responsibility, he showed his utter lack of training for the job. He had a florid face, beneath a receding, sandy hairline; his blue eyes, and the rather petulant expression of his full lips, did nothing to lend strength to it.

He cleared his throat. "Now look, Jesse," he began uneasily, "I'm not taking sides in this, you understand. But I must say I've heard stories about valley beef being eaten up there on the bench."

"You may have heard right," Jesse agreed, coldly. "I'll admit those folks are kind of careless as to brands, when it's a matter of killing a beef for meat. They figure a steer's a steer. But running off twenty head at a time—" He shook his head. "That's rustling. It ain't their way."

"I wouldn't know anything about that," Rickart said. "What I do know is that you've stayed away from that bench crowd for a couple of weeks now, ever since the night you came back with a knife cut on your ribs and your eye bunged up. Frankly, I think it would be a lot better, all the way around, if you kept out of this."

The words had such a familiar ring that Jesse couldn't keep his glance from lifting, in quick suspicion, to the woman on the porch. The look he got from Blanche told him the truth. She had been working on George, planting an idea in her husband's mind and then letting it grow there until he believed it was wholly his own.

Jesse remarked, coldly, "Sounds like you're giving an order."

"I wouldn't like to put it that way," his boss evaded, uncomfortably. "The fact remains that you're in a position where anything you do is sure to reflect on me, and on this brand. Under the circumstances—"

"Say it plain, George! Are you telling me that if I so much as try to defend my dad and my brothers against a false rustling charge, I'm through at Broad R? Is that what you mean?"

"Don't go putting words in my mouth!" Rickart's face

was flushed now. "I like you, Jesse. I like you enough that I haven't let your background stand in the way of our friendship. But damn it, I can't afford to compromise my position in the valley! I was hoping you'd understand all this."

"I think I do." Deliberately Jesse straightened, taking the reins. "Nobody can make your decision for you, George. Mine is already made!" Without another word, he pulled the buckskin around and sent it out of the yard.

When he sighted Mathison and the others, they had halted their horses at the margin of a seep that watered a small, tilted stretch of pasture. This apparently was where the cattle had been stolen. Both Mathison and Dave Clevenger were dismounted, the latter squatting to study the rain-softened ground. Roy Shull had remained in saddle with a knee hooked around the pommel, in a slack and indolent pose that altered only a little when he caught sight of the rider moving toward them. He must have grunted a warning, for Lorn Mathison's head jerked and he was staring darkly at Jesse when the newcomer rode up.

Clevenger, too, straightened to his feet with a worried look. He was a whole head shorter than the other rancher—a stubby, ineffectual little man, marked by an intense earnestness.

It was Mathison who spoke, clipping the words, his taut anger barely controlled. "Well, Craven! You're going to stick your oar in this thing, are you?"

"I figure to," Jesse answered flatly, and turned his look to Dave Clevenger. "What do you make of it, Dave?"

The little man shook his head unhappily. "Damned if I know. There's the sign," he said, and pointed to the plain hoofmarks in the boggy ground. "Only a couple of hours old. Mathison says they'd already followed it far enough to tell that it heads straight toward the bench."

"That's his opinion! I'll have to be shown."

Jesse caught the small movement Roy Shull made, straightening out of his slouch. Shull's words were quiet but as cold as ice. "You weren't invited, Craven—"

"No—let him come." Mathison formed his decision quickly. "Maybe we can give this boy proof that will convince him, and shut him up." He threw Jesse a challenging look, while the gunman acquiesced wtih an indifferent shrug. Jesse ran his glance across the three men, and nodded curtly.

"I'll take the chance," he snapped. "I'm ready to ride."

Without further discussion, Mathison and Clevenger both turned to their saddles.

As they broke into movement the Spade Bit owner took the lead, and Jesse let him. The sign was definite enough. It pointed east, just as Mathison said. A hard knot settled in Jesse's belly. It looked like Dade and his tramp friends—Pete Horn and Arch Suttle. And if it was, and they got caught at it, they could bring disaster on all the other people on the bench.

They kept moving in a silence unbroken by talk. The land was roughening now as they approached the high fault scarp and the hills closing in the basin on the east side. Sign would have become more difficult to read after they got into the first outcroppings of granite, had the trail not been so very fresh. The rustlers were really pushing their jag of stolen beef, trying to make distance. Still the pursuers, being unhampered, had little trouble keeping pace and they were even cutting down the time a little.

Then, with sudden abruptness, the trail brought up against the heel of a cedar-crested hump of rock, where two possible routes split. Here they reined in.

Escape to the bench lay directly ahead, by way of any of the slanting ravines long erosion had gouged into the face of the red-rock scarp; but the cattle thieves hadn't taken that. Their trail swung instead directly north, over ground that quickly got rougher as it slanted up to meet the first of the heavy timber.

"Well, Mathison?" Jesse prodded him. "They aren't headed for the bench at all. They're taking the stuff through Mule Ear Pass and into the hills!"

If the Spade Bit man had been shaken it was only for an instant. He shrugged and said, "Naturally! They're planning to sell that beef in one of the silver camps back in the mountains—no trouble at all for them to get rid of it there, regardless of brands."

Craven's jaw muscles bunched. "But you will admit this means anybody could have done it, and not necessarily the bench people?"

"I admit nothing. I mean to see proof!"

"Let's keep moving," Dave Clevenger broke in, uneasily. "Handling cattle will hold them back. There's a chance we can catch them, but we'll have to do it before they clear the pass."

Mathison cocked a wry look at the angry Jesse. "You game to try, Craven?"

"Why not?" the other retorted. "It's what I came along for."

An hour went by. The way lifted sharply, now, toward the black mantle of timber that smoked under the sun in slow, hanging trails of rising cloud vapor. They rode in silence, because the trail took all their attention. They followed up into a pine forest and the fog settled on them and drifted among the wet, dark trunks. Rocks and needle litter, slick underfoot, began to give the horses trouble.

Jesse soon regretted that he had not bothered to switch his saddle to a fresh mount before leaving the ranch. The buckskin was tiring badly, and much as he hated to push the horse he didn't want to suggest stopping to rest their mounts; they were on too close a margin. He knew the Spade Bit men would interpret anything of the sort, coming from him, as an attempt to hold them back and let the cattle thieves escape.

It was Dave Clevenger who finally called a halt. The horses were blowing badly, their wet hides steaming and legs trembling. The men got down and walked around, to let them rest. They were high enough that the air held a keen knife edge despite the sun. The trees hemmed them in and laid their heavy scent upon the stillness.

Roy Shull pointed to cow droppings in the trail, and made his first comment since they had started their ride. "We can't be far behind them. How close are we to this pass?"

"Too close," grumbled his boss, who had protested against the halt even though the horses could not have lasted much longer without it. "They're going to snake through just ahead of us. Once they do, we won't have much chance of catching them."

Jesse, having looked his buckskin over and decided it was still in fair shape, had dug up smoking materials and was building a cigarette. He licked the tab and smoothed it down. "You listening to suggestions?" he asked Mathison.

Mathison's stare was hostile. "Well?" he grunted.

A jerk of the head indicated a spine of rock that loomed above them. "There's a trail along that ridge," he said. "The cattle couldn't have made it, but our broncs will if we're careful. It'll save us half an hour, drop us down into the pass just about the time they hit it. Maybe even a little before."

He knew Mathison didn't believe him. To keep a check on his temper he went through the studied motions of snicking a match alight against his thumbnail and touching it to his cigarette. Mathison's lips twisted beneath the heavy mustache, but before he could speak whatever sarcastic thing was on his tongue Dave Clevenger interrupted.

"Jesse here savvies these hills as well as any man alive, I reckon," Dave said positively. "I'll wager he knows what he's talking about."

"You will, eh?" Mathison was able to speak with a sting of contempt that whipped red heat through Jesse; but before he could rise to the bait the rancher added, "Well, Clevenger, we'll take your word for it," and turned away to his horse. They all mounted, first checking cinches; as Jesse fumbled with the latigo, his hands were unsteady, both from anger and from growing uneasiness.

He was resigned to its being his cousin Dade they would find at the end of this. He wouldn't let himself think any further.

They rode again. This faint deer trail was poorer traveling than he'd remembered; the horses, already badly used, were quickly in trouble, and Jesse could feel a crawl of sweat as the buckskin stumbled under him. They had climbed out of the pines now and into fir, and they were being forced to rest their beaten mounts at ever closer intervals.

Then at last the trees thinned, and they came down a bare ledge of rock with the wide pass below, flanked by the mule ears of slick rock that gave it its name. There was no sign at all of recent passage. The winds blew here, stripping the hard rock surface clear of dirt; iron shoes rang as they came out upon this and reined to a halt. As the animals stood and dripped lather from their flanks, the men looked at one another.

And then Roy Shull grunted, sharply, "We just made it! Here they come!"

They were not a moment too early. The plod of hoofs and the protesting lowing in the throats of a small bunch of cattle were clearly audible; seconds later they swung into view around a point of rock. They were Mathison's beef, right enough. They came at a shuffling trot, with heads bobbing; behind them coiled ropes slapped against saddle leather and a man's voice rang thinly, chousing the reluctant animals ahead. Now the riders themselves came through the pine shadows, out upon the bare level of the pass into recognition range. Jesse's heart sank as he saw Arch Suttle and Pete Horn.

But the third rider wasn't Dade! It was a range tramp like the others, a man Jesse had never seen before. He could hardly believe his eyes, or accept the sudden trembling relief that flooded through him.

They came ahead, moving slowly, their eyes searching from beneath the shadows of their hatbrims. Jesse saw how they switched their lasso ropes to their left hands, to leave the right ones empty. They rode spread out, as the stolen cattle moved on through the windy pass and the waiting riders stood and let them come into pistol shot.

Mathison told his companions, tensely, "Wait for your cues!" But even as he spoke, something gave the warning.

Maybe it was the gun that Roy Shull had already drawn half from its holster, or perhaps one of the rustlers had recognized Jesse, or seen the Spade Bit horses matching the brands on this stolen beef. At any rate, a yell went up with startling abruptness, and next moment the rustlers were trying frantically to turn their horses.

Jesse never knew how the shooting started, though he guessed that Shull might have been the first to get a ready gun into the open. Ropes of flame spurted, and the volleying gunfire mingled with the bellow of frightened cattle and the ring of iron shoes on bare stone. The tired buckskin shied like a startled cat, nearly unseating him; he cursed it, and got his own cedar-handled Colt out of the holster and tried to settle on a target.

He fired at Pete Horn and saw the hat go kiting off his head; shooting from the saddle of a frightened bronc, there was little real chance of hitting a moving target. The guns seemed to be working of their own accord, like a chain of firecrackers. The twenty Spade Bit steers were in a frenzy; some tried to turn back, while others came charging madly, straight ahead through the swirl of powder-smoke, the gleam of their swinging horns adding to the terror of the horses.

Then something struck Jesse on the upper arm, a blow that might have knocked him off the saddle if his other hand, clutching the reins, hadn't saved him. The buckskin reared on trembling legs. He yelled at it, hoarsely, and as it came down to earth again he looked at his hurt arm. Blood was beginning to show.

He realized numbly that he'd lost his gun. It lay on the ground, glinting back the sunlight. With one dogged purpose, he got out of saddle and went after it, somewhere finding the sense to remember to hold onto the reins, or the buckskin certainly would have bolted. His fingers were without any feeling and they refused to work for him at first when he stooped and scrabbled after the fallen weapon. Then he got his hand on it, and straightened to look around.

But the fighting was over.

In a flurry of pounding hoofs the rustlers had left the scene of battle, heading back down the pass road; Shull and Mathison were spurring after them. Now they, too, had vanished, and the steers were scattered. The wind swept the stink of the guns out of the thin, chill air and, looking around, Jesse discovered that he and Dave Clevenger were alone.

Dave, his face white and running with sweat, came close and leaned from the saddle, still holding his gun in a hand that trembled with excitement. "You're hurt!" he exclaimed.

Jesse shook his head. The numbness hadn't yet left his arm and he could not feel the pain, though it would be starting soon. But it looked to him as though the bullet had slicked only through the fleshy part of the arm.

The main thing he felt was the lightheaded sense of relief that they hadn't found Dade here with his friends.

He dropped the gun into his holster, and with the other hand began to fumble at the knot of his neck cloth. Clevenger, seeing what he was trying to do, put up his own gun and hastily dismounted to get the cloth free. Then he wrapped it tight just above the wound, to halt the sluggish flow of blood.

They were just finishing this work when Lorn Mathison and his gunman came riding back from the pursuit. "They scattered," Mathison answered Dave Clevenger's question. "Hit for the timber and we had to let them go." He looked around him at the windswept, empty pass. "Now we got to chouse those steers out of the hills before they can get clear away from us."

Clevenger told him, "You'll have to do that job by yourselves. Jesse got an arm drilled in the shooting. I'm taking him down to let the doctor work on it."

It seemed to be the first that Mathison realized someone had been hurt. He stabbed Jesse with a look, whose meaning was veiled. He looked at the blood that soaked the man's sleeve. Then he grunted something, dismissing the matter, and swung down to make a quick haul at the cinch strap of his saddle. He smoothed the saddle leather with a sweep of his hand, drew his gun and looked at the loads which he had already replaced. He was starting to mount again to head after his cattle, when Jesse challenged him.

"Well, what about it, Mathison? Are you convinced?"

The Spade Bit owner turned slowly. "Should I be? Because you got hit? That could have been an accident. Far as I got any reason to believe, those were part of your bench crowd. They looked about like the breed."

"They weren't!" snapped Jesse.

"Far as I'm concerned, they were."

He started to turn. Anger sent Jesse's hand out, to take him by the shoulder and pull him around again. There was a swift, almost silent whisper of metal on leather; he saw the flick of motion from a corner of his eye, and when his head jerked about he saw Roy Shull's gun out of the holster and lined directly down at him from the gunman's saddle. He almost gasped in disbelief. He had never seen Shull draw before—and he had never seen a draw with the flashing speed of that one.

Slowly, he dropped his hand, as Mathison moved his shoulder to dislodge it. There was a moment of tense silence, broken only by the sweep of the wind across the pass and the blowing of their tired horses.

Then Dave Clevenger spoke, and his voice held firmness. "I know all the Cravens by sight, Mathison, and most of the others. I can tell you that those three were strangers to me. And anyhow, I hold Jesse's word good!"

Mathison turned slowly to look at him. His voice was still hard, but he could not dismiss Dave Clevenger with a sneer. The Spade Bit man said heavily, "Is that so?"

"Any time! I think he's proven his point. In fact," the little man added, and his voice was hard as he looked at Mathison's angry face, "I suspect that you owe him an apology for the charges you've been making against his people."

The other's chest lifted on a sharp breath; his dug-in

cheeks took on color. "The hell I do! I'll never apologize to that cut of swine—not about anything!"

Despite the pain in his arm, thawing and throbbing now as the bullet shock leaked out of it, Jesse took a step and reached for him. Just short of his target he heard the snick of a gun and remembered Roy Shull and the Colt muzzle trained directly on him. He heard Shull's deadly warning: "Back up, Craven! Lay a hand on him and I'll kill you!"

He checked himself, to look first at the gunman and then at Shull's employer. The muzzle of the gun was a black and menacing thing. Sensing then that feelings were too high—that nothing could be settled now without tripping the trigger on them—he forced himself to back away. At the same moment he was hit by nausea from the pain of his arm.

That must have showed in his face. For at once Dave was saying, anxiously, "Let's get going, Jesse! We have to get that arm tended to!"

Reluctantly, because he was too physically weak just then to resist, he turned his back on the Spade Bit men and let Clevenger lead him, stumbling a little, to his waiting mount.

Chapter Five

Doctor Paul Talbot finished his work on Jesse's bullet wound in short order, and told him that except for a stiffness that would wear off in a few days, he was good as new—except for a ruined shirt. Before he and Dave Clevenger left, Jesse asked the doctor to look in on his sister the next time he was up on the bench, explaining that Ellie was going to have a baby. Doc Talbot asked no questions, which was typical of the kind of man he was; he said he'd be glad to call on Ellie.

When they got outside the office, Dave Clevenger said, "We don't see much of you these days, Jesse. I know you're busy, but Catherine and I were wondering why you don't drop out for dinner some time?"

Jesse shot him a sharp look. "Catherine? Why, she doesn't have any use for me, Dave. She wouldn't want a roughneck tramping mud across her living room!"

Clevenger's prominent ears turned faintly red at the

charge. "She's not as bad as her bark," he insisted, stammering a little. "Really, she likes you."

"Oh, sure!" Jesse laughed, too harshly. He added in all seriousness, "I'd like to believe it, Dave—I really would. And I wish I could take you up on that invite."

"Try it, then, some evening. We'd be glad to have you. Honestly."

But Jesse, remembering Catherine Clevenger's aloof, cold manner, remained wholly unconvinced; and he showed it. He let the subject drop without making any promises. And a few minutes later, Dave Clevenger mounted and rode out of town.

Jesse stayed around a bit. He bought a new work shirt to replace the one that had been ruined, and switched into it, with a few grimaces of pain as he got it on over the injured arm. Afterward he stepped into the Colorado Bar, finding the place empty of customers, and had a solitary drink while he took time to think things over.

Even if Mathison had recovered that twenty head of beef, he wasn't going to be satisfied. He'd been so damn sure, this time, of managing to pin something on the bench people! Now he'd be looking harder than ever—it was up to Jesse to make old Bob and the rest take the matter seriously. He'd have to convince them Mathison meant business.

Seemed as though he had been in a continual bind since he took over the foreman's job at Broad R. Had it been a mistake, then—his coming down here to the valley? Long as he stayed one of the easygoing Cravens, he'd never been like this. And the trouble wasn't ended. Right now the time had come when he must quit this stalling, and ride back to Broad R to see if he had a job left.

A little this side of the ranch was a place where the road took a twist and a dip, and dropped suddenly into a thinly wooded swale. He was approaching this when Jesse heard, across the afternoon quiet, the shrill whinnying of a horse. He dragged the buckskin's reins, fumbling for his gun.

He could not see the trail ahead, but a dozen alarming thoughts chased each other through his mind—of Roy Shull, and of Dade and the three range tramps he'd helped trade bullets with that morning. Suppose Horn and Suttle hadn't pulled out, following the shooting; they might still be somewhere near, waiting for a chance to get him alone.

But then he decided, with a grunt of self-disgust, that his nerves were simply edgy. Deliberately he shoved the gun away and gave the buckskin a kick. The trail rounded a boulder and dropped away across a flinty lip of rock. And below him he saw that other horse, a roan, grazing on dropped reins near the edge of the timber; it lifted its head and trumpeted again, shaking out its mane, as the buckskin came into sight.

Seated on a rock, in an attitude of comfortable waiting, was Blanche Rickart.

That it was Jesse she had been waiting for became clear the instant he appeared on the trail above her. She looked up, and at once rose gracefully to her feet. He could not avoid the meeting. He clucked his tongue at the buckskin and went down the trail. A breath of dampness came from the trees, and cloud shadows rolled across the earth, brightening and darkening. Blanche stood motionless, watching him. She was dressed for the saddle, in half boots and a tight-fitting blouse, a fringed riding skirt that snugged closely to the curve of her hips and waist. A flat-crowned hat with a whangleather throatlatch hung between her shoulders, leaving her blonde hair free to the sunlight and the tug of the wind.

She was, Jesse had to admit, a woman to whom the strong sunlight of this rough land was kind, setting off her beauty but seeming to have no effect toward roughening or burning her fine skin.

He rode up and halted, not dismounting, simply staring at her and waiting for her to say the first word. What she said was, "I've been worried. They said you were hurt!"

Jesse raised his right elbow, let it drop back. "My arm? It's nothing. But who told you about it?"

"Why, Mathison—and that gunman of his. They came by afterward."

"And told George what we ran into?" He shook his head. "I'm plumb surprised Mathison would have the gumption to admit he made a mistake—though I suppose he knew Clevenger was bound to spread the true story." He added, "Mathison get his cattle out?"

"He was going to send some men up to find them and bring them back."

"I see." He hesitated, fiddling with the reins and debating whether to ask the next question. "And did George—

did your husband say anything more about me? About firing me?"

Instead of answering him, she said, "I want to talk to you, Jesse."

Something cautioned him, making him reluctant to get down or to spend more time here alone with her. But he could not very well refuse, and so he came out of the saddle to stand before her, the reins in one big hand. He said, "Yes, Mrs. Rickart?"

"I asked you to call me Blanche," she reminded him.

"That's right."

"You don't need to worry about the partnership," the woman went on, quickly. "George didn't really mean what he said. And he knows now it wasn't your family that took those cattle. If there're strange riders in here, running off Spade Bit stock, they could do the same thing to us any time. George sees that. He sees that he needs you around, more now than ever!"

Jesse told her, "That's a load off my mind, about the partnership. Naturally, if anybody takes a grab at Broad R beef I'll stop them, if I can. Don't matter who it might be. I mean that."

"I know you do."

His exhilarating satisfaction over her news was tempered by a strong desire to end this interview. Blanche saw that he was about to turn back to his saddle and she stopped him, placing a hand on his wrist. "Do you have to be in such a hurry? I've been waiting for nearly an hour."

"For me?"

"I can't believe anyone is that blind!" she exclaimed. And then, moving a step nearer: "Haven't you even noticed me, in all these months?"

Jesse had turned suddenly cold inside. Curtly he answered, "You'll have to excuse me," and swung away, reaching for the stirrup.

The tone of her voice halted him. "If you want this partnership," Blanche said, very quietly, "you won't turn your back. Not to me!"

Very slowly he came around, feeling a masklike stiffness come across his facial muscles. "That sounded like a threat!"

"No, no!" the woman cried, quickly. "I didn't mean it that way! I—Why can't we be friends, Jesse?" Without warning she rose onto her toes, and her arms lifted. A hand moved up his sleeve, to pass behind his shoulders, and touch the thick mat of untrimmed hair curling low upon his neck. She was trying to pull his head down toward hers. Her eyes were half closed, her red lips moist and parted.

Deliberately Jesse reached up and took her hands and pushed her away from him. "This is foolishness," he told her, sternly. "We'll say nothing more about it!"

Blanche's eyes opened wide. She looked as though she had been slapped. "Aren't you even human?" she cried. "Am I as unattractive as all that?"

"You're about the handsomest woman I ever laid eyes on. But you're George Rickart's wife."

"And are you afraid of him?" The woman's lip curled faintly. "What if he did find out? He'd do nothing. He hasn't any spine. He hasn't anything!"

"You must have thought so, to marry him and let him bring you out here from Denver."

She gave an angry shrug. "You wouldn't understand. I was in a spot, and he was the way out. Besides, I hadn't seen you then."

"Me?"

"Yes!" she cried, and her whole manner melted. "You're a man, Jesse! You're the man George Rickart can never hope to be. There's something in you that's strong and independent—like no man I've ever known!"

"Don't you know what that is?" he retorted; it was his turn to let scorn touch his mouth and his voice. "I'm bench folks—don't you remember? One of those roughneck Cravens! We're nothin' but a wild, uncurried bunch of scrubs!"

"Perhaps." She shook her head. "I don't really care. Whatever it is—"

"Whatever it is, I'm asking you to leave me alone. Pick on somebody else! I've worked damned hard to get where I am, and I want to stay there!"

A glitter of danger had come into Blanche Rickart's eyes. "You won't do it by insulting me!"

"Meaning that you'll get me fired unless I—" He couldn't finish it. There was an ugly crawling inside him and his hands had knotted tight. He forced them open, and dragged in a deep breath through set teeth.

"All right. Go ahead, Blanche—if you mean it! You got influence enough with George, I guess."

He thought for a minute that she was going to hit him, and he braced himself to take the blow. Instead she whirled and walked over to her waiting roan. She said, in a voice that was edged with ice, "Hold my stirrup, please."

Without a word he moved to comply.

Her boot toe went into the iron. Her hand touched his shoulder, lightly. Then she was up and gathering the reins —head erect, jaw set in angry firmness; she would not even look at him now. Before Jesse could rise into his own saddle, Blanche was already putting the roan into a lope, and spurring away up the trail.

Neither had known it, but there were witnesses to that meeting. Up on a rim of the swale, where the sound of a horse's whinny had first drawn them, two men hunkered motionless on their ankles, knowing that the stunted cedar at their backs prevented them from being skylighted. For a long time after Jesse Craven and the woman were gone, they stayed like that without speaking. It was Roy Shull, idly dribbling a handful of sandy dirt back and forth from one hand to the other, who made the first comment.

"Very amusing! Did you know that was goin' on?"

Lorn Mathison turned slowly to stab a look at him, and frowned as he read the pure malevolence in the gunman's lidded eyes. "You really think it meant anything?"

Shull gave a snort. "She was waiting for him, wasn't she?"

"But we didn't actually see—"

"It might be interesting to hear what Rickart would think of what we saw!"

Something in the remark brought Mathison quickly to his feet, eyes sober as he stared at the other man. "This is none of our business, do you understand? We carry no tales to anyone!"

The gunman thought that over, and then merely shrugged. He tossed his handful of dirt out across the lip of the rim, where the wind caught and scattered the grains in a glittering swirl. "Sure, sure," he grunted indifferently, rising. "Hell! It's certainly nothing to me, one way or another."

They let it go at that. And yet, there was a new and speculative cast to Mathison's gaunted face as he led the way back to the place where they had tied their horses.

Chapter Six

IT WAS A BEAUTIFUL MORNING. Jesse sat his horse slackly, in front of the post office shack in Bueltown, and flexed his sore arm as he waited for Tom Nealy to come out with the mid-week mail. It was pleasant to have even a moment free of pressing chores. Summer work, here in the basin, was saddle work—long miles of checking stock, of tallying the shape of the grass and pulling bog and riding fence lines. And now that summer was past its prime, already the range was stirring with preparations for the big annual event—the fall gather.

Roundup brought with it redoubled work and responsibility for a man in Jesse's position. This was, he thought, the probable reason George Rickart had made no further reference to their near quarrel, in these days since the aborted rustling attempt.

When Jesse gave his report of the shooting at Mule Ear Pass, the only comment George Rickart had had to offer was, "What's happened once could happen again, I suppose. The three you tangled with sound like ordinary range tramps—and if they are, they've probably had a scare to last them for a while. But, let's keep our eyes open."

"I intend to," Jesse had agreed.

"And take care of the arm," Rickart cautioned him.

That should have been the end of it, but Jesse couldn't believe that his boss had forgotten entirely. He was a strange, moody fellow, Rickart—sensitive about his poor physique and his incompetence as a ranch manager, with a touchiness brewed in him from childhood by the ill-concealed contempt of a hard-fisted father. A man like that would be just the kind to swallow his feelings, to pen them up inside and brood on them during long black hours of sleepless nights.

One thing, at least, was to the good. So far as Jesse could tell, Blanche hadn't kept her veiled threat to make trouble for him. It had been a mistake to put her off the way he had, with the Craven bluntness that said what it thought and gave no mind to the consequences. There was too much depending on his staying here at Broad R—more even than his own future. There were his folks up on the bench, badly in need of a friend at court just now with hostility spreading among the people of the basin. For that reason, he should try to placate Blanche. That he had hardly even seen her since that awkward scene on the town trail, he didn't know whether to count a good sign or a bad one. All in all, this stiff arm of his, painful as it still was, constituted the least of his worries.

A meadowlark, in a field beyond the town, was challenging the high sun, and from the smithy across the street came the slow strike of hammer on steel. Jesse swung his glance in that direction. Suddenly he straightened, unhooking his knee from the horn and shoving his boot into stirrup. He clucked to his pony and rode across the street, out of the warm sun and into the shadow of the shed's wide doorway.

It wasn't Abel McQueen shoeing the horse. The blacksmith sat idle on the edge of the quench tub, watching, legs crossed beneath his apron and huge bare arms folded. The old man who was doing the job had removed his rusty steelpen coat and rolled up his sleeves for it, revealing a set of muscles not yet gone soft with age or disuse. After a few taps on the shoe he'd selected he picked up a rear hoof of his ribby chestnut and tested the fit. Not satisfied, Luke Wigfall shook his head and tossed the shoe back into the barrel and fished up one he liked better. He dropped this into the coals, and was reaching to work the bellows pull when he first noticed Jesse sitting his saddle, beyond the door.

He sang out, jovially, "Well! Good morning!"

"Morning, Parson," said Jesse.

The old itinerant had a mind like a bear trap. He saw a good many people, riding his lonely circuit through the hills—a Bible in one pocket of his saddlebags, an ancient six-shooter in the other; but he never seemed to forget a face, or the name and the history that went with it. He said now, "And how's your family, Brother Craven?"

"Tolerable. At least, they was when I saw them three weeks ago. You haven't been up to the bench?"

"Not yet. I aim to go directly I finish here." Wigfall picked up a rasp, and turned to work on the hoof while the iron was still heating. His balding head, with its straggle of lank gray hair reaching to his collar, gleamed as he bent to the task.

Jesse formed his decision quickly. "If you don't mind, Parson, I'll ride up with you. There's a job waiting."

"A burying?" the preacher asked, in quick sympathy. "Not old Bob, I hope?"

"Ain't anybody dead. I'll explain later. How long will this take you?"

"No time, no time at all," the parson assured him. "I only wish I was as skillful savin' souls as I am at shoeing a horse. I try to keep my hand in, son. I figure if the Word ever fails me, I'll still have a trade."

"I hope the Word's good and strong in you this morning," Jesse answered, dryly. "We got need of it."

In order not to have to explain anything more within hearing of the blacksmith, he reined away and crossed the street again. Tom Nealy was just coming out of the post office, carrying a handful of letters, circulars and newspapers. Jesse leaned from the saddle.

"I won't be heading back just yet," he said. "The parson and me are taking a little ride."

Nealy followed the jerk of his head. Over at the smithy, sparks were being rung now, with clanging blows, from the cherry-hot shoe upon the anvil. The puncher looked back at Jesse, showing a plainly worried look.

"Up on the bench?" he demanded, and got Jesse's nod. "If I'm asked, where do I say you went?"

Jesse felt a stiffening of his jaw muscles. He knew Tom had his interests at heart, but at the thought that he might be expected to lie and conceal his interest in his own people, stubbornness rose in him. "Tell 'em the truth!" he snapped. "This is family business, and I've every right to take care of it."

"Sure, you have," the other agreed quickly. "How long will you be gone?"

"Not too long—" Jesse began; but then a premonition spoke to warn him otherwise, for he amended that to, "I don't exactly know. It may take a while, so look for me when I show up."

He crossed again to the smithy, where he waited, scowling and impatient, for Parson Wigfall to complete his shoeing.

Jesse was a moody companion during the ride up to his father's place. Luke Wigfall didn't appear to mind. This blacksmith turned soul-saver made talk enough for both. He kept it up continually—though Jesse, deep in his own thoughts, would have been hard put to remember, afterward, just what the man talked about. But Wigfall did not demand an attentive audience for his monologue. An occasional grunt satisfied him.

When they came in on the Craven place no one was immediately in sight except for Jesse's younger brother Billy, sunning himself on a bench by the shed door. The moment Jesse and the parson came in view Billy let out a shout and tossed aside the harness he was mending. He was a boy of nineteen who had nearly the full Craven height, though he still needed filling out. He ran to take the bridles of both horses, and Jesse demanded, "Anybody around? Where's Pa, and Homer?"

"I'll go chase 'em down," Billy offered.

"You do that, soon as you you've taken care of the parson's bronc. Step down, Wigfall," Jesse added, "and make yourself at home." He set the example by swinging out of his own saddle, wincing just a little as his tender arm pulled on him.

Billy was leading the chestnut away when his mother came out, smoothing her skirts self-consciously as she greeted the minister. Ellie appeared in the door, but stopped short when she realized her brother hadn't come alone. Jesse, seeing her, called gruffly, "Go put on your good dress, carrot top—it's your wedding day!"

He had told Wigfall nothing except that there was a marriage to perform. Now the parson turned, and laid a stern and disapproving eye upon the girl. Hot tears of shame sprang to Ellie's eyes and caused her pretty mouth to tremble. He was himself all too conscious of the beginning swell of his sister's slender figure, but he had tried to keep his eye from it. Now, really angry, he whirled on Luke Wigfall.

"You're here to make it right," he snapped. "Go fix yourself up pretty, Ellie." To the older woman he added, brusquely, "Make the parson comfortable, Ma. I'll fetch the bridegroom."

A moment later he was mounted again, and heading to find Dade Haggis.

There was all the difference in the world among these places scattered along the bench. Each was touched by poverty, but it did seem that anyone with decent self-respect could avoid living in squalor. Some, though, were enough to make even Jesse understand Lorn Mathison's withering contempt for the people up here. And the shack where Dade Haggis lived was one of the worst.

Dade's father had run off, years ago, leaving no one to do the chores except Dade and his slattern mother. As a result, for the most part they didn't get done. Thought of little Ellie being brought here to wear herself out doing the work for the worthless pair of them hardened Jesse's mouth as he pulled rein in front of the crude board-and-batten shack.

There were shingles missing from the swaybacked roof, and the screen door was punched through. A litter of trash and empty cans filled the yard. From a pen behind the house rose the racket of the pigs that were Ma Haggis's pride and joy. Otherwise the place seemed deserted, and seeing no movement at the windows, Jesse sang out impatiently. At last a slapping shuffle of carpet slippers whispered across the bare puncheons, and Dade's old mother showed herself in the doorway.

She was a rheumy-eyed, gaunted female, with a wrinkled hide that was blotched exactly like the skin of a frozen apple. She put one gnarled hand against the side of the door and demanded, "What do you want?"

"I'm looking for Dade."

"You won't find him here," she promised, wagging her head. "You're too late."

Jesse stared. "What do you mean, too late? Where is he?"

The old woman made a hopeless gesture. "Took off, just like his pappy before him."

"I don't believe it!"

"Come and see for yourself. He packed everything he could tote. His guns, his clothes; what little grub we had. Stripped the blankets off his bed. Have a look if you don't reckon it's so."

Numbly Jesse slid out of the saddle and, leaving his reins trailing, followed her inside. He stood in the middle of the filthy clutter, looking around him. He saw the empty wall pegs where Dade's gear had hung, the rifled bunk in the corner.

Behind him the old woman continued her whining lament. "What have I ever done to rate a pair of no-goods like them Haggises? Father and son, they been nothin' but a hardship to me! Saddle me with his child and then go off and leave me with the raisin' of him—that's all the old man ever managed to do. And now that I'm old and need to be taken care of, that Dade—"

"When did he leave?" demanded Jesse.

"Early this mornin'," she stammered, her complaining cut off. "Him and those lowdown tramps he picked up with."

That made it all suddenly crystal clear. A moment only Jesse hesitated, and then he nodded curtly and said, "All right. Thanks!" and whirled and walked past her, slamming through the screen door.

As he was fumbling for the stirrup, stabbing his toe into it and lifting into the saddle, her voice followed him. "You see him, Jesse, you tell that worthless cousin of yours he better be getting back here. I don't like the looks of his friends. He'll go bad, Jesse! He'll wind up at the end of a rope, or worse. You tell him, from me!"

He rode off without looking back, and the shrill sound of her voice was lost in the racket from the pig pen. He muttered under his breath, "I think you're wrong. I'd say your boy's gone bad already!"

He'd have to have a fresh horse, he decided; depending on how much distance Dade had on him, he might be in for a long chase. It never occurred to him for an instant that he might consider letting the man go. He turned his buckskin in the direction of his dad's place and gave it the spur, anxious to waste no more time than could be helped.

But it was already close to noon when he dismounted at the shed and began hastily stripping saddle and gear off his sweating horse. There was a skewbald gelding in the adjoining corral that was his brother Homer's favorite mount and, Jesse knew, had the bottom to carry him a considerable distance over the mountain trails. He roped it out and switched his saddle to it, and then led the mount over to the house.

His mother saw him from the window. She came out, carefully letting the screen go shut behind her so it wouldn't jangle. Her puckered eyes studied his face.

"Why didn't you fetch Dade with you?" she demanded.

"He's cleared out, Ma. For good, it looks like."

Her face turned tragic. "Oh, no!"

"Maybe he got wind about the parson, and left before I could come for him." Jesse laid a hand on his mother's shoulder. "Now, don't you worry. It ain't getting him anything, I promise you that."

"You're going after him? Oh, son, be careful! I don't want—"

"It's got to be, Ma. For Ellie's sake. Afterward it don't matter a damn to me where he goes or what happens to him. I gave him fair warning he was to be here today— that I'd fetch him back if he tried pulling out beforehand. I aim for him to know I meant just what I said, even if I have to drag him in at the end of a lass rope!"

The woman's strong hands knotted, twisting at her apron; she silently shook her head, her eyes anxious on the grimly determined face of this tall son of hers. But she had no argument.

Jesse asked, "What's the parson doing now?"

"We been sitting in the house, talking."

"Keep him there. Don't let him get away from us till I get back."

But when he started to mount, her protest came suddenly. "You just can't do it, son! What if Dade puts up a fight, and you with a hurt arm?"

That held him for an instant. "How'd you know about my arm?"

"Why, the doctor told us—the one you sent up to look after Ellie."

"I didn't know he'd been here. What does he say? Is she gonna be all right?"

"Of course she is."

Jesse flexed his arm, not letting the sore stiffness be reflected for her anxious eyes to read in his face. "Well, so am I. This isn't anything. Near good as new."

He saw no point in telling her that he would have two others to face besides Dade Haggis. Before she could argue further, he got the stirrup and swung quickly into the saddle.

"Won't you even have something to eat before you go?"

"No time," he grunted, lifting the reins.

"You wait right where you are, do you hear me?" Lifting her skirts, she headed for the kitchen. Jesse started to call after her, then gave it up with a shake of the head. His mother was gone only a matter of minutes, but to his impatient awareness of the slipping away of time it seemed longer. He knew she was right, however, and that there was no judging how long it might be before he would have another chance at food.

When she returned she had a huge sandwich of cold

meat and thickly sliced bread. Jesse leaned to take it, saying, "Thanks, Ma. And you best not say anything to Ellie." Afterward he jerked the reins and kicked the skewbald, and the fresh horse started under him with a lunge.

He looked back once, with a wave of the hand that held the sandwich. He was already starting to work on it as he rode at a brisk canter out of the yard.

Chapter Seven

HE DIDN'T NEED INSIGHT to guess that the pass road was the one he wanted. That was the direction Dade's friends had tried to take their stolen beef, a week and a half ago; it was the one quick route through the hills, and into the spine of the Rockies. If Dade had broken over and decided to go on the loose with his tough friends, the free flow of wealth in the big silver camps would be a lure. West lay only cattle range, and the badlands of Utah. And Jesse knew they wouldn't have gone out by way of Buel Creek.

He cut across the red-soiled, cedar-broken benchland, making directly for the lower reaches of the pass trail. He hadn't been riding more than a few minutes when a horseman appeared out of some timber below him and came up with a shout and a wave of his hat, and Jesse eased in on the reins to wait as he saw it was his brother Billy.

Red dust spouted under the bronc's braced hoofs as the kid pulled in and demanded, "Where you bound for, Jess?"

"Nowhere," he grunted shortly. "Did you locate Pa and Homer?"

"Yeah, I found 'em. They'll be along home directly."

"Then you get on back and stay with Ma. I got an idea she'll be needing you." Not waitng for an answer, Jesse kicked the skewbald ahead.

But a moment later, to the sound of the other bronc following hard after, he twisted about and hauled rein, glaring. "I said to get home! That's an order!"

"You ain't orderin' me!" his brother retorted indignantly, pulling up beside hm. His manner quickly changed, however, became pleading. "Tell me what's up, Jess! Why you heading into the mountains in such a lather?"

"It's none of your business."

"The hell it ain't!" Suddenly, the kid's eyes widened. "Hey! You fetched that parson with you. I bet you're looking for Dade Haggis!"

Jesse drew a sharp breath. "Ma never told you—"

"Naw, she didn't tell me anything. But I—well, I heard her and Ellie talkin'. And, there was that fight you and Dade pulled off. I'd been wondering a lot about that. I just sort of puzzled things together.

"I'm no kid, Jess; I have an idea what goes on. And Ellie's my little sister, same as she is yours. If Dade Haggis is running out on her, I want to help bring him back. Look! I got my old gun, in case we need it."

Jesse frowned, intending to refuse but knowing it would do no good. Billy wore a determined, set look just now that was very familiar. These two had been very close from childhood up—there was a bond between them, such as had never existed between Jesse and the silent Homer. It was perhaps due to this, and to a sudden, stabbing realization of how far he and this younger brother had drifted apart lately, that Jesse heard himself saying with reluctance, "All right. But don't get in my way, and don't slow me down! We're probably in for a long, tough ride, if it isn't already too late. You understand?"

"Sure," said the other, a quick grin splitting his face.

He needed no other invitation; he was already kicking his dun saddler into motion, and setting him at Jesse's stirrup.

The dust of the pass trail showed hoofmarks, fresh enough that Jesse knew they must have been made some time that morning: three horses, moving toward the timber. He had no proof that these were the same riders he was pursuing, but neither did he have any doubts. With characteristic Craven stubbornness he pushed ahead, playing out his hunch as he saw it.

Billy kept looking at his brother, his eyes dubious. "I count three of them," he said presently. "Would that be right?"

Jesse nodded curtly. "Why? You getting scared?"

"Scared?" The other colored a little, and his lower lip thrust out. "Aw, Jess!"

"I'm just kidding." Relenting, Jesse began to tell the kid something about the men Dade was trailing with; and that led to a brief account of the run-in up here at the Mule Ears, a week and a half ago. It was a long time since the two of them had had a serious talk. Jesse filled his brother in on a lot of things he thought he should know. The kid had sense, for one so young. He asked questions and his expression was deeply sober as he considered what he had just learned about Lorn Mathison and the rancher's growing threat to the bench people.

Here at least, Jesse knew, was one member of his family who would take a warning seriously, and give it the thought it deserved.

At the summit of the pass they dismounted and loosened cinches, to give their horses a blow. The scent drawn from sun-warmed fir needles was strong about them as they waited; but when they pulled up the straps again and began easing into the descent of the east slope, they rode into shadows—the sun dropping behind them now, low and curtained by the ridges. Realization that afternoon was slipping away spurred Jesse anxiously.

Aware of the cool wind that stirred the timber and dried the sweat out of his shirt, he began to understand for the first time the odds that were against him. He ran a real risk of losing this chase altogether, if the forest night should come down before he could overtake the man he was after.

This side of the pass was unfamiliar territory. There was no business that would bring him this way, normally; the last time he could recall having been in here was some years ago, on a hunting trip with old Bob and Homer, and he had only a dim recollection of distances. He wasn't expecting it when just at sundown the trail skirted a timbered knob and then dropped abruptly away toward a rich, open park below him.

Fine graze was down there, and the glint of water. Hemmed in by flanking ridges, the park reached northward like a pointing finger; and despite the gathering smoke of dusk Jesse could see the horses spread out, peacefully feeding off the meadow grass.

A mile or more north of the trail, he made out a pattern of log buildings clustered at the foot of the nearest piney ridge.

Unconsciously he pulled rein, and Billy's voice close beside him asked, "Pellman's?"

Jesse nodded, not immediately speaking as he made his study. The barn and the outhouses were dark shapes, bulking black against the timber. Lamplight glowed at the windows of the main building. Smoke from the stovepipe chimney curled in a lazy ribbon, reminding them of the chill that was already beginning to work into the end of this dying day in the high country. A clump of saddle horses stood tied to palings of the veranda, and Jesse considered these with narrowed eyes.

It was too far to distinguish markings, or even tell the number for sure; but he thought he counted three.

"This is Pellman's, all right," he grunted, answering Billy's question. "And just about where we might have expected to catch up with them!" All at once there was a growing excitement, and with it a wonder that this place should have slipped his mind. Had he remembered, he would have been much less uneasy about Dade getting away from him. Perhaps, on the surface, this did have the look of nothing more than an isolated horse rancher's spread. But occasional rumors that floated across the hills said otherwise.

"I got to see those broncs," he muttered half to himself. "Find out if one isn't Dade's sorrel."

A dim wagon track left the main trail, to cut over toward the roadhouse; but they didn't take this. At Jesse's lead, they turned their horses into the jackpine and instead began working along the slope that way, holding in the cover it gave them and paralleling the side road farther down. It was dark here under the trees, and the horses had trouble in the loose silt. But it was the one way of moving in close without being seen by whoever might be at the house.

Jesse listened to the sounds of Billy following close behind, and was aware of a queasy tightening in his stomach. It wasn't fear of men like Dade and his tramp friends, though there'd be three of them to face; but he wasn't accustomed to this sort of business and he didn't like it. He found himself flexing his sore arm, troubled by the handicap of its continuing, painful stiffness. As he came in closer to the buildings he halted from time to time, listening, hearing only the wash of the wind through pines that stood thick and black against a darkening sky.

Finally he reined in and swung down to the needle carpet, anchoring his lines to a tree trunk. Billy did the same, and when they went ahead on foot they suddenly found the house directly below them.

Jesse held up at the edge of the trees, studying the clearing for sound or movement. They had used so much time that it was very nearly dark now, but enough gray light remained to show that no one was moving around outside the buildings. The heavy log walls muffled any noise from within.

"You keep an eye open," Jesse muttered. "I'll drift down and look at those broncs."

To keep the house above the snow level, deep here in winter, it had been built up the slope a little distance. Its forward end, with the railed porch fronting it, was raised on log pilings. Jesse watched the windows and the back door of the long, low building, as he broke into the open. He thought uneasily of dogs, but he had no sign of any; he got to the house without rousing an alarm. Hugging its rough logs, he quickly gained the front of the house and there ducked under the raised porch, to pause for a moment, listening. After that, as he crept forward, the tied horses caught his stealthy movements and they stirred restlessly.

It was too dark to see much. Such light as fell through the door and the front windows didn't reach beyond the edge of the porch. Jesse hesitated, reluctant to do this; then, with a fatalistic shrug, he dug up a match and struck it alight against a piling.

As the flame sprang to life he lifted it high, sheltered by cupped palms, and swept it in a wide semicircle. The light flickered and wavered. Just in front of him a horse jerked its frightened head; an eyeball gleamed with a brief ruby glow.

The match guttered out and he dropped it, from habit setting a boot on the blackened stick. It had been only a moment, but he had seen enough. One of those three horses was Dade Haggis's long-coupled sorrel.

Next instant Jesse's grunt of satisfaction stuck in his throat, as a startling scrape of cloth against wood brought him quickly around. His hand found his gun and fumbled it up. Tight nerves might have started him shooting at the next telltale noise except for Billy's anxious whisper: "It's me, Jess!" And all at once trembling, Jesse lowered the gun.

"Kid, you damn near got yourself killed!" he exclaimed, under his breath. "Why didn't you stay where I told you? Haven't you better sense than to—"

Billy didn't seem even to hear the scolding. "Is it Dade?" he asked, moving up to join his brother.

"Yeah, it's Dade, all right. Now all I got to worry about is walking in there and fetching him out without a shooting. Won't do Ellie any good if I have to tote him back dead."

"Why not let me try?"

"You? Don't talk foolishness! Just be quiet a minute and let me think."

"I mean it!" Billy caught at his brother's arm. "You go in that door, all three of them will dig for their guns. But they don't know me from Adam."

"Dade knows you."

"Yes, but he won't start shooting. If he sees me it will just confuse him—likely throw them all off guard."

Poking around the edges of the idea, Jesse saw sense in it. It fit in with his opinion of Dade, and those saddle tramps. "There's a back door to the place," he observed. "If we can manage to put them in a whipsaw, they might none of them try to fight. But it's a risk."

A chair scraped overhead; boots tramped across the puncheon flooring. These sounds helped prod him to a decision. "All right," he said. "We'll give it a try. But for Pete's sake don't rush things!"

Fear that the kid would be overanxious and not wait for him to set the trap made Jesse hurry. His head banged against a timber, nearly stunning him and shaking down dust; then he was out from under the building, the loose soil of the slope dragging at his boots as he climbed it at a quick run. Above him, stars were pinpointing the sky that was turning from beaten silver to the full black of night. Cherry sparks streamed upward, like other stars, from the stove pipe chimney jutting from the roof. Jesse reached the door in the back wall, and sucked in his breath on finding it fastened.

The delay was only momentary, however. Searching fingers located the latch string, and he cracked the panel open. After a moment he pushed it wide enough to slip through, and closing the door held up there in darkness, his shoulders against the wood as he listened.

The voices he heard came from beyond a second door opposite, covered only by a skimpy curtain. Enough lamplight spilled past to show him that the room he stood in contained an unmade bed and a table and chair, and odds and ends of clothing hanging on wall pegs. He went across it soundlessly. His gun was still in his hand, and as he flattened himself at one side of the inner doorway he used the barrel cautiously to push the curtain out of the way an inch or two.

He looked straight into the eyes of Dade Haggis.

It was so startling that it all but unnerved him, until he saw that Dade was not really looking at him but at another man—Arch Suttle—who sat opposite, on a bench that ran the length of a crude deal table.

Pete Horn sat next to his partner, and at the end of the table, teetering on the rear legs of a chair, was a third man Jesse decided must be the horse rancher, Jim Pellman himself. He had a half-Indian look about him—coarse black hair, and smoky eyes under a shelf of heavy brow.

One other person was in the room, a disheveled woman who worked about the big wood range dishing up beef and beans. She had served the guests and was just handing her husband a steaming plate which he jerked out of her hand without a look or a word.

"If you leave early," the horse rancher was saying, "you might hit Three Creeks tomorrow night. That should put you into Silver Lode by next day or the day after. A wide-open camp, I've heard."

"One of the workings struck 'em a new ledge, a month or so back," Pete Horn said with his mouth full. "You know what that means—money floating, fools trying to get rid of it. Plenty of women—"

Jesse saw Dade Haggis nod, over a forkful of meat. "By God, that's for me! A man's crazy to waste all his time in one place, like I have. I should of thumbed my nose at this country a hell of a long time ago."

"Just stick with us, boy," Pete Horn told him, wagging his ugly head. "You wait! We'll show you the ropes. We'll show you things you won't believe."

At the far end of the room, the plank door had started to open. Leather hinges squealed, or maybe it was a draft of chill air stealing in that carried the warning. Jim Pellman was the first to turn his head; his chair slapped the floor as his whole body jerked forward. Pete Horn looked up and dropped a knife into his plate with a clatter.

Billy gave the half-open door a solid kick and strode boldly in, the door slamming so wide that it hit the wall and rebounded. The kid stood framed there with a tight, scared grin on him and gun gleaming, as he tried awkwardly to cover the whole room at once.

And at the same instant a sweep of Jesse's arm ripped aside the curtain.

Everyone except Dade Haggis being concerned with Billy's entrance, it was Dade who caught sight of Jesse. The blond man stared wild-eyed at him across the littered table.

"Get 'em up!" Jesse ordered, above his leveled gun. "I mean it! We got you two ways, Dade!"

He knew it was touch and go. The pair that had their backs to him scrambled around and then froze at sight of the gun, with bewilderment giving place to something uglier as they recognized Jesse. Down at the end of the table, the half-breed Pellman hunched his shoulders and one of his hands slid from the table, out of sight. But Jesse caught the movement; instantly his gun swung on the man. "Bring both hands out where I can see them," he snapped, "and lay them on the table."

Pellman obeyed, but his face was black as thunder. "Who are you?" he demanded in a hoarse voice. "What the hell do you want?"

"From you, nothing. We came after one of your guests. Billy," he added, flinging a reminder at the kid, "you watch them now—good and careful!"

"I'm watchin', Jess!"

Jesse moved forward quickly. As he circled the long table, Dade shifted position to watch him. The blond man's eyes were belligerent and a muscle leaped in his craggy cheek. "You mean me?" he shouted hoarsely. "What makes you think I'd go anywhere with you?"

"You'll go." Jesse answered coldly. "A month past, I said I wanted you to stick around until a certain piece of business could be taken care of. I warned you what I'd do if you tried to leave."

Subtly, Dade's expression changed as understanding hit him. The hostility altered, became tinged with mockery that lifted a corner of his mouth, and brought a snicker out of him. "So that's it! Don't make me laugh, boy! I got more important things to do just now, than makin' an honest woman out of some little—"

Jesse hit him. It was a stinging, backhand blow that jerked Dade's head and wiped the sneer off his face. Dade loosed a hurt bellow and would have lunged to his feet, but Jesse tapped his shoulder with the gun barrel. That held the man.

"Sit still!" Jesse ordered, in a voice that trembled with anger.

The words, and the threat of the gun, were meant equally for the other men around the table. He stood and glared at them, and Arch Suttle quietly put back the hand he had removed from the oilcloth. They sat like that while Jesse got a hard control of his fury. Then he told his cousin in a quieter voice, "You'd best go ahead and finish your meal, Dade. You've got a long ride ahead of you tonight."

He was suddenly conscious of his own emptiness, and remembered his kid brother, who was watching all this in awed silence. He turned to the woman by the stove and asked, "Is there enough of that grub to dish up a couple extra plates?"

She only stared at him, and then looked at her husband for instructions. The half-breed settled his head lower between his shoulders. "This is my house——" he was starting to say, darkly, when Billy Craven's sudden shout of warning cut him off.

"Jess! Look out!"

His brother hadn't caught the sound of the rear outside door opening; he didn't see, until too late, the figure that moved into view where that curtain had been yanked aside. As Billy's cry brought his head up, he saw the man now and recognized him—remembered the affair at Mule Ear Pass when there had been a third cattle thief riding with Horn and Suttle. Jesse had forgotten him, but he must have been outside and seen a prowler entering the house by the back way. At any rate he came with his gun in his hand, and a shot disrupted the tail end of Billy's outburst.

Probably it was Jesse's quick turn that saved him. The bullet missed by a few spare inches. The shock of it jarred along his nerves; the gun he was holding kicked his palm, while the men seated between him and the doorway yelled and hurled themselves wildly off the long bench to the floor, out of danger.

They left a cleared space between, and through the sudden, eye-smarting film of powdersmoke Jesse watched the man in the doorway begin to crumple. Had anyone else tried to reach a gun just then, he couldn't have prevented it. He could only stand in a kind of horror and watch the man he'd shot sag against the edge of the door. The hand that held the gun opened; the smoking weapon swung for an instant by the trigger guard before it slipped off his finger and clattered to the floor. He lit on his face, and rolled over onto a side and was still.

Jesse realized suddenly that he had quit breathing, that bands of iron were beginning to tighten about his chest. He drew a long, shuddering gasp, and then the nausea hit him.

He dragged his eyes away from the crumpled body, and looked around. They were all staring at him. No one broke the silence that followed the crashing of the shots. Even the sullen breed had taken on a look of shocked respect, and Jesse saw fear beginning to show on the faces of the others. Contempt for them settled in him, and helped take the edge off his horror at what he had been forced to do.

He said, coldly, "I guess now you know I mean business! Finish your meal, Dade, so we can be leaving. Billy, fetch the lady a couple of plates and let her fill 'em."

Billy swallowed. He said, in a thick voice, "I—I don't reckon I'm hungry, Jess!"

"Eat while you got a chance," Jesse ordered, sternly, and the kid gave no more argument. No one in that room seemed now to want to question his word.

Chapter Eight

THERE WASN'T ANY PURSUIT, although Jesse expected it. As deep night settled he kept an ear tuned for hoof beats on the trail, but silence claimed the hills. The three of them did little to break it. They rode spread out, Billy ranging ahead and Jesse bringing up the rear, and Dade silent and sullen between them.

Dade had given no more trouble; Jesse had taken his gun away from him and also appropriated the rifle off his cousin's saddle. For a while he held the weapon cradled in the bend of his unhurt arm. Later on, as muscles began to cramp in the night chill, he tied the rifle to his saddle.

He thought he understood what had happened. The killing had had its effect on the remaining pair of saddle tramps and sapped any appetite for vengeance. As for Dade, they seemed to have abandoned him to his fate. And Dade knew this; it showed in his heavy, sullen resentment and in the way he obeyed orders, with no argument.

It was the condition of the horses that dragged him out of his preoccupation, and warned him that they couldn't keep up the pace. The mounts needed rest, even if the men could do without. And so he called a halt, briefly, and an hour afterward ordered another. But then he pushed them on, mounting to the pass, and down out of fir and into pine again. The last miles were little more than a crawl. By this time the horses were completely played out, and Jesse's skewbald gelding had picked up a limp that held them back even more.

Gray dawn was taking on light and color and the old rooster in the Cravens' chicken yard was making a lonely, creaky crowing when at last they drifted, ghostlike, into the yard—three men who were pale with fatigue, their horses stumbling under them in the last stages of exhaustion. They drew up, and the other two looked at Jesse.

He ran a palm across his mouth, feeling the scrape of whisker stubble. His eyes felt as though they had been reamed from his head with hot pokers. The home place slept, peaceful and quiet in the dim morning, with shreds of fog clinging to the boles of the pines above the clearing. He dragged in a long breath, and lifted his shoulders in a futile effort to work some of the aching tiredness out of them.

He nodded toward the silent house. "Everybody's still asleep," he said, his voice subdued in the hush of the dawn. "Don't have to wake 'em up just yet. Let's take care of our horses."

But Dade, for the first time since they left Pellman's seemed on the verge of balking. He cleared his throat and said hoarsely, "Listen to me, damn you!"

Jesse didn't give him time to finish. "Get down," he ordered, with tired impatience. "And put up your sorrel. He's been carrying that saddle long enough." Dade peered at him in the dim light, and seemed to debate with himself as he ran his tongue across his lower lip. Then, scowling heavily, he kicked his weary bronc and pointed it toward the barn.

Jesse looked for the parson's horse, and found it in one of the stalls; this made him nod in relieved satisfaction. Depend on Ma to do her part and keep the old man here until they got back. Knowing Luke Wigfall's restless habits, he was sure it had been no small task. Well, the thing was all but accomplished. A few minutes, a few words of ritual,

THE OUTLAW BREED 63

and the harm Dade had caused Ellie would be remedied as far as possible.

The horses stripped and cared for, Jesse gave the blond man a cuff on the shoulder and motioned him toward the house. "Let's go, Dade, and get it over with. You got nothing to be sore about," he added testily, seeing the look his cousin gave him. "We want nothin' from you except your name, for Ellie's baby. After that, I'd just as soon never have to lay eyes on you again."

Dade's mouth worked on dark, unspoken thoughts; his fists curled but went slack again. With a shrug, he turned and, no longer protesting, walked ahead of the other two.

The yard was showing the first flush of sunrise.

When they entered the neat house, Jesse noticed that the room was still warm from last night's fire in the cookstove, and he could guess a little from that how long into the night people here must have waited. Now the family slept, likely worn out with waiting.

Jesse let his brother close the door behind them. He motioned with a nod of his head toward the stiff chairs ranged about the oilcloth-covered table, and told Dade shortly, "Sit there. I'll see if there's anything left in the coffeepot."

While Billy stood at the door, as though too tired to move another foot, Jesse scaled his sweat-marked hat onto a wall peg and walked over to the stove. He took up the pot, judging its contents with a swirling motion, and finding it still nearly half full he proceeded to shove kindling and wood into the box and dropped in a lighted match. As fire started to roar up the pipe he reset the lid and moved the pot forward to heat. He was just turning the damper when the door of his folks' room silently opened and his mother came out, pulling a faded wrapper over her nightgown.

There was a shadow of fear in her eyes that faded as she looked from one to the other of her sons and saw that they appeared to be all right. Her glance moved finally to Dade Haggis, slumped in a chair by the table, and it hardened in chill dislike. Dade's answering look was hostile and insolent.

She turned to Jesse, then. "We didn't know what to think," she said.

"I know," he said, and added, "Where's the parson, Ma?"

"Upstairs. We put him in Billy's bed."

Jesse turned and threw a look at the youngster. "Go fetch him down." Billy nodded and went to the steps to the loft and began to climb them. Jesse told his mother, "Better tell Ellie to get ready."

She stared at him. "You don't mean right now—at this hour in the morning?"

"As good a time as any," he grunted. "Get the thing over and done with."

His mother shook her head and told him, anxiously, "You're worn out, Jesse. Your thoughts ain't tracking right. Let me fix you some breakfast, and you get some sleep and then—"

"Coffee will do me fine," he interrupted. "And I got no time for sleeping. I was due back at the ranch last night. I won't put this business off a minute longer."

She saw he was inflexible, and said, quietly, "All right. I'll call your sister."

The day and the house were coming to life, now. The light was stronger at the eastern window, steam from the coffeepot rising across it. Jesse moved to fetch down a couple of cups off the shelf. He heard a stirring around in the loft overhead as Billy wakened the sleeper—the gruff, male murmur of voices up there and then the stomp of a boot being rammed home. He took the cups and the coffeepot to the table, poured black liquid into the thick china mugs and pushed one roughly toward his cousin. Dade looked at it sullenly, picked it up and tossed the coffee into him.

Jesse was replacing the pot on the stove when the bedroom door opened again and old Bob came out.

Jesse said, "Hello, Pa."

Bob scarcely saw him. His eyes had lit on the face of Dade Haggis, and he stopped suddenly and stood there with a stern and dangerous look on him, his thick chest beginning to swell. "So you fetched him back!"

"Yeah," said Jesse. "Ma's waking up Ellie. We'll have the preacher down here directly and settle this once and for all."

"That's proper!" Fury swept aside all trace of Bob's usual good humor. He took a sudden pair of strides that carried him to the table, and he leaned across it and twisted his fingers into Dade's shirt and lifted the man bodily out of his chair.

"You skunk!" he whispered, tightly. "You hear this, and you hear it straight! I'd gladly strip the hide off you —but instead they say I got to stand by and see you married to Ellie! Well, all right. But once it's done you get off my property and stay off. I ever see you again, it'll be a hard day for you. You follow me?"

Dade didn't flinch. His face, inches from Bob's, kept its insolent sneer and he said coolly, "Take your hands off me, old man!"

Bob shook him furiously, despite the weight of the younger man. When he let go of Dade and slammed him back into his chair, Bob was panting and nearly sobbing in his rage.

Then they heard the clomp of boots, as Homer Craven came tramping down the ladder. Homer was an ugly bear of a man; he had inherited all the strongest Craven features and they hadn't blended well—the high-bridged nose, the broad cheekbones, the blunt, solid jaw that came from Ma's side of the family. He looked like a heavy-handed brawler, but he had the mildest nature of any of the clan. He came scowling to Jesse now and demanded, in a troubled tone, "What's this the kid says about a fight at Pellman's?"

Jesse made a face. "Billy shouldn't have told you. He always did talk too much."

"He says you killed a man—"

"Look, it's nothing for Ma to hear. She'd take it hard, and she's got enough to worry her. I'll tell you about it later," he promised. Homer, though unsatisfied, let it go at that.

Billy came down, then, saying, "Parson's gettin' dressed. How about some of that coffee?"

All these big men seemed to fill and dwarf the room. It never occurred to any of them to sit; or perhaps the Cravens chose to remain aloof from Dade Haggis, who still hunched over the table, nursing resentment. The rest stood about with coffee cups steaming in their hands; and presently the door of Ellie's room opened and all the men turned. Maud Craven appeared, followed by her daughter.

Ellie halted on the threshold as though afraid to enter. She looked small and pale and, to Jesse's mind, prettier than he had ever seen her. Her brown hair was carefully brushed and caught back with a ribbon that matched her only nice dress—a dress Jesse had bought her. The dress was a poor fit now; it showed too clearly the changes that nature was beginning to make in her young body. Jesse felt the mask that settled stiffly over his face. And yet at the same time, looking at his sister, he was aware of something that had been felt by other males before him—the astonishing beauty of a pregnant woman.

She looked shyly at her brothers, and then her glance rested on Dade Haggis at the table. Their eyes met for a moment, before his slid away and he turned his head. Jesse saw his sister's mouth tremble.

Very quickly, then, the ceremony took place. They moved the table back to make room, and Ellie and Dade took their places before the parson. While wood fire popped and crackled in the stove and morning light grew, Luke Wigfall read the words of the ritual. He did a perfunctory job, his manner soured from the enforced delay and the unearthly hour. Surrounded by Ellie's menfolk, Dade went through his part in sullen acquiescence.

There was no ring, of course. When this lapse brought an awkward moment, Maud Craven hesitated only an instant; then she stepped forward and shoved at Dade the thin gold band she had worn for nearly thirty years. "Use that," she said, curtly, and watched as Dade took it and put it on Ellie's hand.

"Pronounce you man and wife," the parson said, and snapped his Bible shut.

Jesse felt easing of long tension, and with its passing the tiredness set in. He saw Ellie turn to Dade, looking up into his scowling face, her own doubtful and yet expectant. But there was no chance for Dade to kiss her, even if he had been so minded. For now old Bob stepped briskly forward and his hand struck his son-in-law's shoulder, turning him. Bob said, "All right! That's all you're wanted for. Now, get out of my house, and don't dare walk inside it again! Never, do you hear?"

In the silence that followed, Billy let his mouth open wide on an audible yawn. "Damn, I'm bushed!" he told the room. "I'm gonna climb into the hay and catch up on some sleepin'."

Jesse, too, had had all of this he wanted. He had dug a few bills from his pocket, which he shoved now into the parson's hand in payment for his trouble. He paused for just a moment at Ellie's side, and laid a hand on her shoulder in a gesture of silent understanding. She tilted her head up; he caught her miserable look and the flash of tears in her eyes.

Afterwards he had got his hat off the wall and without a word to anyone he walked out into the blue-gold brightness of the new morning.

A fury was on Dade Haggis; he spurred away from the Craven place without regard for the punished state of the animal under him. On a rise, just before the dip of the ground hid it from him, he twisted in the saddle and looked back.

The sun was clear of the hills now and its light struck the shakes of the house roof, bouncing up at him as from a mirror and causing him to squint painfully. He sat there for a long moment, hating all those people. He had found his saddle gun in the barn, where Jesse had left it, and now he drew it out, tempted to slam a couple of bullets defiantly into that sun-bright roof. But he shrugged and, slapping the rifle back into the scabbard with the heel of his palm, straightened around again and gave the tired sorrel a hard kick forward.

The sorrel carried him across the ridge, and the Cravens were left behind—but not Dade's sense of wrong and indignity.

As he rode he cursed them all, though the main force of his resentment was reserved for his cousin Jesse. Jesse was the whole source of his humiliation. First, licking him in a hand-to-hand, and then riding after him and shaming him in front of his friends—dragging him home like a kid caught playing hooky! That made a score that couldn't be let stand—and someday he'd settle it.

He shrugged away the scene at Pellman's. Jesse had had the breaks, and taken advantage of them. Next time he wouldn't have it all his own way.

For now, though, Dade knew things were running against him. They'd married him off to Ellie, for all the good it was going to do them, or her either! Dade salved his ego with a sneer.

The main thing right now was that they'd put a finish to all his plans. He'd thought to have seen the last of this stinking bench country. He'd found himself a bunch of saddle pals that he could go a long way with—men who knew the country east of the hills, who'd been around and knew how to help themselves to what they wanted. Now he didn't kid himself that he'd ever see Pete and Arch again.

A beat of hoofs interrupted his thoughts and brought him around, turning his horse and dropping quickly out of the saddle on the bronc's far side. Cautious and narrow-eyed, he laid a hand on his gun and waited for that horseman to show himself.

For a moment there was nothing to see. The running horse hit a stretch of scab rock and the drum of its hoofbeats was flung briefly across the silence, to be muffled again in loose soil. Then, down out of the scrub pine and cedar, the rider burst into view—and it was Ellie.

The tension went out of Dade, but his expression was sour as he walked around to the head of his horse and took the reins. Standing there, he let the girl bring the animal to a sliding stop. She was still in her wedding dress, skirts kited up above her knees so she could ride astraddle. Her legs were brown and bare; her hair had come undone in the wind of the hard ride and she jerked her head up to put it back across her shoulders.

Balanced in front of her on the saddle, Dade saw now, was a bundle tied in an old quilt; he looked at this and demanded heavily, "Where do you think you're going?"

"With you."

Dade gave a sour grunt. "Like hell!"

"You're my husband now, Dade!" Her face was twisted with the pain his words gave her. "Doesn't that mean anything?"

For answer, he merely shrugged and moved to take the stirrup. "Dade!" she cried. In a quick movement she slipped from her horse and came to him. Her mouth was trembling and the tears glistened on her cheeks. She was very pale.

"Don't turn your back, as if you thought I'd—tricked you into marrying me! Believe me, I never would have said a word to anyone, except for the baby."

He wouldn't look at her, and he made no answer. The morning sun beat down strongly on them, surrounding them with the odor of baked saddle leather and horse sweat, and the pine scent that rode down the morning breeze.

"Now that it's done," Ellie went on, in a small voice, "I want to be a wife to you, Dade; a good wife. Please give me a chance—let me come with you, to take care of you and make a home for you and your child. Don't you love me even a little, Dade?"

The touch of her hand on his sleeve seemed suddenly to loose a fury in him. He whirled and his arm came up, in a crosswise, chopping thrust. It struck Ellie across the side of the face and she was knocked off balance and twisted and fell heavily.

"Let me alone!" Dade shouted. "I never want to lay eyes on you! Go back where you come from!

"Go back to the Cravens," he repeated, his voice rising as all his piling anger boiled over, "and tell them something for me. Tell 'em I was meanin' to leave this country—to clear out of it for good. They wouldn't let me; they dragged me back. All right! Now people around here may have more of me than they ever wanted! You tell 'em that!"

Ellie lay crouched on the ground, her face hidden by her coppery hair and her slender shoulders heaving with sobs. Dade glared at her a moment, too angry to feel shame. He turned, then, and got into the saddle and struck off at a deliberate canter. He didn't look back.

Minutes later he broke out of a screen of cedar scrub and, as a sloping meadow opened below him, reined in suddenly. Down there, a few cows and their calves were feeding along the bank of a muddy creek; from where he sat he could see the Cravens' C Bar brand on them.

That wasn't all he saw.

He kneed the buckskin nearer, easing down the slope. On the far bank of the stream, old Bob Craven's bull lifted his head once, looked indifferently at the rider and went back to his feeding. He made a target no one could miss. Dade Haggis swallowed, his throat gone tight, and reining up he slid his rifle from the scabbard.

He thought the first shot was wide. The smoke filmed out and the bull still stood on braced legs, ugly head lowered. Frowning, Dade grunted and levered another shell into the chamber, put the gun to his shoulder again. He was lining up the sights when the bull suddenly crashed to the earth.

Dade's lips pulled back from his teeth in a grin. Deliberately he pumped a second bullet into the carcass, and a third. Afterward, lowering his gun, he looked at the bull lying yonder with the blood beginning to puddle as it leaked from his nostrils.

He said aloud, "We'll see how they like that!" Satisfaction was already swamping the resentment in him as he shoved the gun away, and yanking his weary horse around he kicked the spurs home. He was even whistling a little, tonelessly, as he rode.

Chapter Nine

Doctor Paul Talbot, observing the noon quiet over Bueltown, saw those three horsemen come in off the bench trail, and he sensed at once that trouble rode with them. The horses were dusty and looked hard-used, and the men themselves—Bob Craven and his sons—had a grimness and purpose about them that carried unmistakably, even to the window of the doctor's second-story office.

They caught Talbot's interest and held it as he watched them ride into the street below. Almost directly under his window they drew rein; Homer said something and indicated the Colorado Bar across the street. His father shook his head, but the negative was not very adamant. Talbot saw the old man drag a palm across his mouth as he considered the cool and inviting darkness beyond the slatted swing doors.

After that all three went through the pockets of their patched jeans, fishing up odds and ends of change. Old Bob pooled their resources in a horny, cupped palm, and Talbot watched him count the coins. He appeared satisfied with the result; he nodded, and at once the three men were kneeing their horses across the street and swinging down in front of the Colorado Bar's long hitch pole.

For a moment the doctor hesitated; then he turned from the window and went out through his office, down the narrow stairs, and across the sun-lazy street. The saloon was empty except for the three from the bench. Talbot waited until the bartender finished pouring their drinks and collecting the mound of small change that old Bob solemnly pushed forward in payment; then the doctor caught his eye and nodded toward the beer pump. A mug was filled, collared, and spun into his hand across the wet surface of the bar.

The Cravens noticed him and there was an exchange of nods. Talbot watched the men drain their glasses slowly, savoring every drop. He drank half his beer and set it down while he wiped his mouth on a pocket handkerchief. He said pleasantly, "How's my patient?"

Old Bob cocked a look at him. "Ellie?" He shrugged, his manner short and cranky. "Fair enough, I guess." He twisted the empty shot glass in his fingers, eying the inside of it as though hoping to find some drop he'd missed. "Good whisky," he observed, "if it is expensive. We don't often get a chance at this town stuff."

"I don't know when was the last I saw any of you fellows down here," the doctor observed casually. "You celebrating something?"

The question, idly put, earned him a quick flashing stab of the old man's eyes. It was Homer who said, as he slapped his own glass down onto the bar top: "Ain't likely!"

Young Billy, having downed his shot with as much gusto as the others, turned now to throw a question at the man behind the mahogany. "You got any idea where we'd be apt to find that Mathison hombre, on a day like this?"

"Mr. Mathison?" The bartender looked from one to another of the trio, his eyebrows lifted. "Why, out at his ranch, I suppose. Most all the outfits are busy getting ready for next week's roundup."

Bob said, "Reckon that's where we'll look, then."

"You have business with Mathison?" Paul Talbot asked.

The old man gave him a slow and careful look. "Yeah. We have. A little matter of a bull."

"It ain't anything you'd know about, Doc," big Homer said. "I suggest you forget it."

Billy grunted impatiently, "Come on! Let's go!"

Paul Talbot stood and watched them tramp outside, the beginning of a troubled frown on him. The bartender muttered, "Something's sure chewing that bunch!" The doctor, not answering, pushed his beer away unfinished and dropped a coin onto the wood, afterward crossing to the door and standing there, just inside, to see the Cravens jerk reins loose and swing into the saddles. Old Bob, he noticed, was as agile and sure of movement as either of his sons.

They mounted, and rode out along the valley trail, and purpose was plain in the stern look of them.

Across the street, the liveryman's gangly kid had brought a dappled bay into the barn doorway and was using a currycomb on it, working with thorough and loving care. On an impulse Paul Talbot left the saloon and walked over there. The boy straightened as the doctor entered the barn, and the man asked him, without preliminary, "That a good fast horse?"

"Fast enough, Doc," the youngster said with pride. Next moment he made a practiced grab and caught from the air the flashing coin that Talbot unexpectedly spun at him.

"Here's a silver dollar. I have another for you if you can find Jesse Craven in a hurry."

The boy said, "I reckon I can. What do you want with him?"

"A message. Deliver it and report back, and the dollar's yours."

"I'll find him. Name your message."

Talbot said, "Tell him he'd better get to Spade Bit and get there fast! His father and his brothers are headed that way, and it looks as though they mean trouble. Something about a bull."

The youngster was already throwing a saddle blanket on the bay. "Don't spend that cartwheel, Doc. It's practically mine."

Spade Bit headquarters was a fair measure of its owner's ambitions. It was a big one, a fully equipped plant, with stock barns and hay barns and two bunkhouses, and a system of tight-built, heavy-timbered corrals. The house looked twice as big as any a bachelor could need, a solid structure built half of stone and finished with unpeeled logs, and with a deep veranda fronting it beneath the jut of a flat, low-pitched roof.

The Cravens, feeling no awe of the wealth all this represented, rode at a hard clip beneath the high gate and came into the yard; they did not slacken speed until they were almost at the house, and then they yanked reins and brought their horses to a plowing halt, at the very edge of the porch. While the horses milled restlessly, tearing up the sod, old Bob shouted, "Mathison! You inside there? If you are, come out!"

Getting no immediate answer, he swung his head impatiently and sized up the activity of the place. Preparations for roundup had the home ranch occupied. Yonder, at the corrals, the horse herd was being shaped up; the ring of sledge on steel issued from the blacksmith shed where shoes were being replaced. Closer at hand, the cook was supervising a couple of helpers as they made repairs to the underpinnings of a chuckwagon. They had the wagon blocked up, its box tilted at a steep angle so they could work on it. Just now they had left off their labors and were staring at the trio of horsemen, startled by old Bob's shout. Bob yanked his horse around and went tearing over there, his sons spurring at his heels.

The punchers backed away a little, but the cook stood his ground, arms akimbo and wind whipping the apron about his thick, wide-planted legs, as the newcomers hauled rein and their restless horses dripped sweat into the dust. "What do you three savages want?" he demanded harshly.

"Your boss. Where is he?"

"You got business with him?"

"It ain't your affair if we have or haven't," Bob retorted. "You answer my question."

"Go to hell!"

Old Bob showed his teeth, then, in a crooked grin. "Why, thanks! I kind of thought that's where I could find him!"

He swung a glance around, and it took in the blocked-up wagon and sharpened wickedly. Suddenly with no sign or warning of his intentions, the old man drove his horse forward. A boot came out of stirrup; old Bob placed it against the bottom edge of the wagon box, and kicked.

A smaller man couldn't have given the needed leverage, even with the rig hoisted at that convenient angle. There was a startled yell from the three Spade Bit men and even the burly cook broke and scrambled as the wagon started to go.

It crashed to its side and rolled on over, in a splintering of bows and rip of canvas. A jerk of the reins pulled Bob's horse back, then, and his right hand was on the butt of his holstered gun as he watched the men, challenging them with a wolfish stare.

Billy had already drawn his weapon and was holding it tight and ready. Homer, turned suddenly cautious, was squinting toward the smear of sunlight on the corral timbers. Somebody was coming this way at a run, spike-heeled boots lifting small, wind-torn streamers of dust.

But now, at the house, an angry shout sounded and they looked around quickly. Lorn Mathison himself was there, leaning across the veranda railing. He was staring at the wreckage of the wagon, at his three crewmen standing helpless, at the guns in the hands of the trio from the bench. He gripped the railing and the graying hair whipped about his face as he called harshly, "What's going on?"

Bob Craven yanked the reins; deliberately turning his back on the cook he kicked the horse and drove straight toward the house again. His sons followed, Homer with a last anxious look behind him for the Spade Bit men. Old Bob seemed to have dismissed them completely; he rode straight up to the veranda and swung his horse broadside to it, where he could lean from saddle and peer into the face of the owner. "What's going on?" he mimicked, scornfully. "Why, I'd say, Mathison, it looks like somebody smashed up your wagon!"

The rancher's sunken eyes blazed; his cheeks seemed even more deeply hollowed than normally, as though sucked in by the consuming fire that blazed within him. "So you're deliberately setting out to provoke me!" he exclaimed, as though he could not yet believe it. "You mean you've actually got no better sense that to come over here looking for a fight?"

"Uh-uh," grunted Bob, and shook his head. "Not lookin' for one, Mathison. We brought it with us."

"Don't think I won't oblige you." Mathison's voice shook. He straightened from the railing, his back stiff, his hands working at his sides. "If you've got anything to say to me, I'll give you just about five seconds to say it and then get out!"

Bob sneered at him. "Big talk! You knew we'd be here, I reckon. The minute we found him!"

"What do you mean? Found who?"

That brought a scornful exclamation from Homer, who with Billy had ranged his horse a little behind his father's. Old Bob's face had been whipped to livid rage by the question and he answered loudly, "You know all right, damn you! The bull! You said you'd kill him. We never rightly believed you'd dare—not without some excuse, anyway!"

"Are you crazy?" cried Mathison. "I don't know anything about your bull."

"That's a lie! You told my boy Jess you'd do it. Try to deny that you did!"

"If somebody killed the damn scrub," the rancher told him icily, "it was good riddance. I'll waste no more time arguing." And he swung away, his whole body rigid with dislike. He had moved a step toward the door when old Bob's shriek of rage halted him.

"Damn you, come back here!"

Despite himself, Mathison whirled. Bob was leaning tensely in the saddle, all but spurring the sweaty horse up onto the porch after him. Bob's hand had clamped itself over the butt of his holstered gun. For that moment it was like a tableau. Spade Bit men, hurrying up from the barn and the corrals, had halted a distance away to stare as though they had no understanding or will to prevent what seemed about to happen.

Then at the corner of the porch, Roy Shull's voice spoke sharply. "Hold it right there, Craven!"

Very slowly the three from the bench turned their heads. The gunman had walked into the scene without being noticed, rounding the corner and placing himself in a position to cover all of it with his gun. He hadn't bothered to draw, though. He merely stood with his right elbow bent and cocked outward, his fingers spread and the tips of them just resting on the backstrap of the jutting gun handle. He said, "All of you! Get your hands up!"

They knew his reputation. They knew a thoroughly dangerous man when they saw him, too, and being caught that way by surprise knocked the fight completely out of them. Old Bob was the first to move. Emotions battling in his face, he let his half-drawn gun slide back into the holster and, slowly, lifted his right hand shoulder high, his left still holding the reins in tight check. And behind him, his sons hastened to comply.

Billy Craven, however, seemed to have forgotten that he had a drawn weapon in his hand. As he raised his arm, the hot sun struck a smear of highlight from the metal; this caught Shull's watching eyes and jerked his head. Without hesitation the gun leaped from Shull's holster. He swung it up and fired. The shot cracked flatly, jarring the stillness. Billy let out a cry as the smash of the bullet, striking him, spilled him heavily to the ground.

There was a choked sound of horror from old Bob. But he could only stare, helpless, at his boy lying in the dirt—at the blood beginning to stain his clothing. It was Homer who shook free of shock and, ignoring Shull's smoking gun, came quickly out of the saddle. And as Bob scrambled to join him, Lorn Mathison lifted a stern and scowling face toward his gunman. "Shull!" he cried. "That wasn't needed."

The man by the corner of the house looked squarely at his boss. "He had a gun out. He was trying a trick."

"I don't think so! I don't think anything of the kind." Mathison's cheeks grooved deeply as the corners of his mouth settled. "Damn it, sometimes I get the feeling you're just too handy with that trigger!"

Roy Shull was not used to being crossed, even by his own employer. His pale eyes flickered and then narrowed a trifle; his voice was flatly expressionless as he said, almost without moving his lips, "Any time you don't like the way I do my job—"

He didn't get to finish. Bob Craven was straightening to his feet and his face was grim. He sought out the gunman and told him, in a voice that trembled with emotion, "Shull, I don't care who or what you are, or how many men you may have killed. I tell you now that if my boy dies, you'll pay—you and your boss!"

"Oh, hell, Pa!" Homer cut him off, anxious and impatient. "Will you quit wranglin' for five minutes? We got to do something for Billy!"

"He's right," Mathison put in, quickly. "Believe me, Craven, I didn't intend this! But you'll have to admit you asked for it—ramming in here the way you did, hunting trouble. Bring the boy inside, and I'll send for Doc Talbot."

For a moment it wasn't even certain that old Bob had heard. A stunned reaction had settled on him. He looked at Homer, who had lifted Billy out of the dust and was trying to prop the boy's lolling head against his knee. He ran a glance across the silent ring of Spade Bit men that had gathered, his eyes not appearing to see them.

Then he straightened his big shoulders and he said harshly, "Hell with you, Mathison! I ain't bringin' him into your house!" He leaned and shoved a hand under Billy's armpit and hoisted the youth limply to his feet. "Hold him!" he told his other son, and quickly turned and swung back into the saddle. "Now, lift him up to me!"

There was no arguing with the old man. Between the two of them, they managed to get Billy across the saddle. Old Bob held him there, cradled against him, unmindful of the leakage of the boy's blood. He took up the reins as Homer turned away to mount his own horse and catch up the reins of Billy's animal.

Lorn Mathison said coldly, "You know you're being foolish. He'll bleed to death!"

Old Bob's face was completely stern, completely unyielding. Encumbered with the limp weight of Billy in his arms, he got his mount turned and wordlessly the watching men drew back, making room. He rode through them with no look either to right or to left. In utter silence, except for the muffled plod of hoofs, he rode out of the Spade Bit yard, Homer following.

Once free of the yard, Homer spurred to catch up with his father. "Pa?" he called and got no answer. He had to reach from the saddle and grab the old man's arm, before he could bring Bob's head around and get the attention of his brooding, bitter eyes. "Where you goin' with him, Pa? We ought to get him to the doctor, don't you reckon?"

Bob looked down at the boy in his arms. Billy's head, lolling against his father's shoulder, was flushed and feverish.

The old man's mouth set in stubborn determination. "I want no basin people touchin' him," he declared. "We'll take him home!"

Chapter Ten

IT WAS A MATTER concerning roundup that took Jesse Craven over to Clevenger's—a question as to which outfit should supply the wagon this year. They generally worked their neighboring ranges jointly, separating the brands after each day's gather.

Jesse hadn't planned to hit the ranch right at mealtime, but it happened that work delayed Dave Clevenger and he and Catherine were just sitting down to the table when their visitor rode in. Dave was the one insisted Jesse stay, reminding him of his promise to take dinner with them; he refused to listen to any excuses. And though Jesse was embarrassed, Catherine assured him with her habitual cool civility that it would be no trouble putting on an extra plate.

Despite his protests, he somehow found himself seated at the table, and Dave's slim, dark-haired daughter waiting on him.

It was a pleasant room. Like the house itself, it had been

built long ago for Dave Clevenger's young bride, with everything in it done according to her plans. Jesse scarcely remembered her from seeing her in town a time or two, as a boy—a tall, serene person, a woman very like the one her little girl had grown into.

Catherine now filled her mother's place with a calm sureness; the flowered wallpaper from Denver, the frilled curtains at the window and the yellow field flowers on the table, a print showing apples and peaches and other fruit spilling improbably out of an overturned basket—these things all seemed to fit her and express her quiet dignity, though they made her stockman father appear a little out of place in his own home.

Jesse watched Catherine move about the room, bringing silverware and cup and saucer, her slender hand and arm disturbingly near as she poured his coffee and set a plate of beef and potatoes and sweet corn in front of him. When he tried to thank her she seemed to brush the words aside, flicking him a glance of her gray eyes. Her mouth a little prim, she said, "You're perfectly welcome, Jesse." And that was nearly all she did say, throughout the entire meal.

Jesse didn't have much to offer himself, once the business of the roundup wagon was settled. Clevenger gave him a narrow surveyal as they ate, and once he asked a little anxiously, "That arm bothering you, Jess?" The younger man shook his head, absently flexing the muscle. What his friend had read in his face was not pain, but utter tiredness.

Time, for him, seemed to stretch back a long way to the happenings of yesterday—the ride, the affair at Pellman's, the killing. Since coming down from the bench that morning, after the dreary wedding, he'd had a couple hours' sleep, but not enough to replace the drained strength, or revive lagging spirits. Depression still lay on him, and in his present mood he felt as though he would never shake free of it. . . .

His fagged brain kept playing tricks on him. It was as though he could see the man going down, arrested halfway in his fall to the puncheon flooring of Pellman's house, with Jesse's bullet in him; and then, superimposed on that image, the face of Ellie wet with tears and long with misery, as she'd stood and tied herself in marriage to that worthless Dade Haggis. . . .

Between Jesse's moody silence and his daughter's quiet

aloofness, Dave Clevenger had pretty heavy going keeping the lagging table talk alive.

And then a horse was larruping into the yard and a rider piled out of the saddle and stumbled on the porch steps, in his haste to reach the door and pummel it with his fist. Clevenger rose quickly and left the dining room. Jesse heard the murmur of voices, and some unnamed alarm had him pushing back his chair even before Dave said, "Yeah, he's here. I'll call him."

It was the kid from the livery stable in town. His clothes were dusty, and so was the horse that stood on trailing reins. The boy told Jesse, "They said at Rickart's you'd headed over here. Doc Talbot sent me looking for you."

"What's he want?" snapped Jesse.

"He said you should know that your father and your brothers were through town a while ago. They had some drinks and left for Mathison's. They wanted to see him about a bull, or something."

Jesse could only stare at him, for a moment—his dulled brain wouldn't let this news seep through. He asked, finally, "When was this?"

"I dunno, Mr. Craven. I made good time but I looked the wrong place for you." He added, as Jesse merely stood there, "Doc said he thought there could be trouble. He thought you maybe ought to do something."

"Yeah." Jesse shook loose. He found a dollar in his pocket and shoved it into the kid's hand. "Thanks a lot. I'll be getting right over."

He was already turning back into the house for his hat, and saw Catherine in the hall. He said gruffly, "Excuse me for hurrying off."

Clevenger tried to delay him, with a hand on his arm. "What's it all about, Jess? Maybe I should go along. After all, you and Mathison—"

"This is my concern," he answered. "I can handle it."

But a sick dread was piling up in him as he pounded out of the yard, spurring the bay mercilessly and cursing the time he knew it would take him to cover the dozen miles to Spade Bit. There could hardly be any doubt as to what had happened.

He didn't know what he expected to find, when at last he sighted the Spade Bit yard. A first sweeping survey showed him no sign of Bob or the others. There was no one near the house. In the yard, the splintered wreckage of a canvas-topped wagon lay abandoned on its side and caught his curious attention for a moment. All activity seemed to be concentrated by the corrals and the blacksmith shed. Jesse, slowing from his pellmell chase, would have swung wide of the house; but something there caught his eye and he rode over, hauled rein, and leaned from the saddle for a closer look, while his winded, wild-eyed pony heaved under him.

The dark spot in the dust was already turning black, as the thirsty ground sucked it up. But there was no mistaking it, and as Jesse straightened again his face was a bleak, hard mask and a band of steel seemed to have tightened about his chest.

Lifting the reins, he saw the two men coming across the yard—Mathison and his shadow, Shull. Deliberately, and without haste now, Jesse swung his horse and cantered straight toward them. Just before they met his horse and slid down. His legs were a little spread and his head lifted and bent forward; his voice held a poorly contained tremor of fury.

"All right," he gritted. "Let's have it. Where are they?"

The pair had halted, Shull drawing aside a step to put a little space between him and his boss. The gunman's look was secretive and dangerous, and his stance held that professional, ready tautness he fell into automatically at any moment of trouble. It was Mathison who answered, "Don't get your dander up, Craven! They've been and gone. I never knew such a family of wild men! Come tearing in here, wreck my cook wagon past repairing, make a lot of accusations that's got no sense to them—"

Jesse didn't bother to follow his gesture toward the splintered and abandoned rig. His eyes never leaving the rancher's face, he said tightly, "There's blood on the ground back there, Mathison. Who was hurt?" He saw Mathison's front of anger waver before the thrust. Suddenly hard put for the words to answer, the man exchanged a flicking glance with the gunfighter at his side. Jesse saw the look, and understood it.

"Your doings, Shull?" he grunted, turning on the gunman. "I thought as much. You break that damn gun of yours out every time there's the slightest chance, don't you?"

Shull's hand was clamped on the handle of it now. His

lidded eyes flickered as Jesse turned on him; he was not used to taking so direct a challenge. He retorted, "Damn it, the kid asked for it. He had his gun out—"

"Billy?" Jesse's shout was hoarse and strangled. "You shot Billy?"

The iron bands squeezed tight; the simmering fury boiled over and red fire seared his vision, as he moved straight at the gunman.

Shull must have thought he was safe from attack, so used to being treated with respect that he couldn't realize here was actually a man with no fear of him or his gun. Though his hand was on the weapon's grips he made no move to draw it, until Jesse was almost on him; then his sneering face twisted suddenly in disbelief, and his elbow jerked with the smooth and effortless speed of his draw. But it was too late.

Jesse was looking for it, and his left hand took a swift, chopping swing. The hard edge of Jesse's palm caught the gunman's wrist, numbingly, and the weapon that had just cleared holster was knocked spinning out of Shull's fingers, in a blur of blued steel and smearing light.

Then Jesse's forward stride sent him slamming bodily into the other man, driving him backward. Shull nearly lost his balance and stumbled to keep from falling. Before he could get set Jesse slammed him again, and then struck a clubbing blow that sledged into him just below the breastbone. Wind broke from Shull's lips and as he started to double, gagging, Jesse brought up his left fist, slashing the man across the lower jaw.

He was utterly merciless. When Shull made an unaccustomed try to hit back Jesse brushed the fist aside, scarcely feeling it in the rage that swamped every other thought and sensation. He saw Shull's hated face just in front of him, and hit it. There was a soggy, pulpy sound; blood spurted. His left arm hooked again and his knuckles bruised against the side of the other man's skull. His right sank almost to the wrist in a suddenly yielding body.

Shull crumpled and Jesse stood and looked at him, while the fury slowly burned out of him. He turned on Lorn Mathison, then, to find the Spade Bit owner looking a little sick. Shull was stirring and moaning feebly. His nose mashed and face cut and bloodied by his opponent's fists, he was not a very pleasant sight for his boss just then.

"Maybe you've learned something," Jesse panted. "Take

his gun away and this boy of yours hasn't much to lean on."

The rancher had regained his composure. He threw a glance around and placed his crew. They had got wind of the trouble and left their work; they were doing no more than stand and gape, but they were within call and that may have helped his assurance. He told Jesse, coldly, "You took Roy by surprise. It wouldn't happen a second time." Yet Mathison was plainly shaken at having watched his gunman leveled.

Jesse wiped a sleeve across his face, noticing how the healing muscle of his arm pulled and ached. Those unthinking, sledging blows had done the arm no good. "I wouldn't be too sure," he grunted. "If this gunslick has killed my brother Billy—"

"He wasn't dead," Mathison put in quickly. "Not when they left here, anyway."

"How long ago?"

"A half an hour, maybe. The kid looked pretty bad, but they wouldn't let me send for the doctor. The old man picked him up in his arms and they rode out. I think they were headed for the bench."

Jesse considered this, combating the heavy lethargy he could feel settling like lead inside him now that the momentary lift of the fighting had ebbed away.

"You claim you don't know what brought on the trouble?"

"I never touched that damned bull! I know I said I would, if I had any more trouble with him. But if he's shot, it was somebody else's doings."

"Whose? You expect me to believe that, without proof!"

"The hell with proof!" Mathison was getting angry again. "My word's good enough. I make straight talk. I said the same thing to them that I'm saying to you, and you can take it or not and be damned to you."

Suddenly Jesse did believe him. There must be some other answer, though he could form no inkling of one. Perhaps one of Mathison's men had done the slaughter and then been reluctant to admit it, seeing the furore it had kicked up. Maybe even Roy Shull, who was slowly working to a sitting position now and holding both hands across his battered face, blood dripping between his fingers.

Jesse shook his head, shoving the problem aside. "I may talk to you about this again, Mathison," he warned the rancher. "Just now I got my brother to worry about. We'll let the matter lie."

Getting no answer and waiting for none, he deliberately turned his back, walked to his horse and scooped the reins into one bruised fist. It was a bad shock, when he moved to lift himself into the saddle, to find there was no spring in his body—he had practically to haul himself astride, and his arms were trembling when he settled heavily into the leather. Physical reaction from the fight was coming in upon him now; it was proving a worse toll than he had realized, on strength already badly overdrawn.

But pride refused to let him show anything to these men of the Spade Bit brand. Head erect and stern of face, he jerked the reins, spinning his mount, and kicked the spur home. He was already lifting the bronc into a fast running walk as he went out of the yard.

He had ridden only a little way when the full effect hit him. Utter exhaustion nearly put him out of the saddle. His sore right arm, punished by the savage use he had made of it, was throbbing now almost to the shoulder. The aching swelled, and finally he unfastened a button of his shirt and thrust his hand inside the gap, to hold the arm in a makeshift sling. The throbbing eased, after that.

Perhaps he could have managed to overtake old Bob and his brothers, even with the head start they had on him— especially if Billy was badly hurt. But there was nothing he could have done, and instead he put his buckskin into the wagon trail toward Bueltown. He rode deep in the saddle, shoulders hunched, swaying heavily to the steady rhythm of his horse. Once or twice he almost dozed, as the blackness of fatigue settled down around him; each time he roused with a start.

Then he was riding through the long main street of the town, and putting his horse to the tie post that fronted the doctor's office. The dark stairwell rose steeply, and his boots, as he climbed, felt weighted with lead. He reached the top, and then could not remember for a moment which direction to turn to find Talbot's office.

The door, of pebbled glass, was propped open to allow some circulation of air. The doctor, in his shirt sleeves, sat at his desk doing some bookwork. When Jesse showed in the doorway, Talbot looked up and at once screwed the cap on his pen and laid it aside. "You got my message?" he demanded, rising.

Jesse nodded. His throat felt dry and dust-lined. "There was trouble, all right, at Spade Bit. I got there too late to stop it."

"Looks as though you stopped something," the doctor said dryly, looking hard at Jesse, "With your face! It's a mess!"

He lifted a hand, felt the bruise about the size of a half dollar that made a spot of aching soreness. He winced and shook his head; he hadn't been aware that any of Roy Shull's wild blows managed to land. "It's my kid brother, Doc. Shull shot him. Don't know how bad he was hit, but I saw the blood he spilled. Mathison said he thought the kid was pretty bad hurt."

"Well, where is he?"

"I was hoping they might have brought him to you, but I guess they didn't. If he isn't here, they must have toted him home."

"Clear up to the bench?" the doctor exclaimed. "Perhaps bleeding to death?" He made an exasperated gesture and turned away, to open a cabinet and take down his black bag and unsnap it. "Those people are enough to make a man lose his patience," he said curtly, as with swift and efficient movements he began loading the bag with bandages and medicines and the bright, metallic tools of his trade. "There's such a thing as too damned much independence!" He added, over his shoulder, "Bottle and glass in the top right drawer, Jesse. Help yourself."

"Thanks." Jesse didn't stop to wonder how the doctor had known he needed whisky. It took an effort to pull himself away from the edge of the door, where he somehow found himself leaning. He dragged off his hat as he entered, dropped it onto the seat of a chair and opened the desk drawer. The cork gave him some trouble; but he worried it out, filled the glass and set the bottle down. As he lifted the drink he saw that Paul Talbot watched him, frowning.

"Let's see that arm, Jesse. You behave as though it were hurting you."

Jesse shrugged and tossed off the liquor. He scarcely felt the burn of it. "The arm's all right. I just hit a guy with it, is all. Maybe harder than I should have."

"I see." But the doctor was studying Jesse with eyes that seemed to read more there than a face usually shows. He appeared about to ask further questions which for some reason he decided to leave unasked. A troubled frown on him, he snapped shut the catches of his bag, took his narrow-brimmed hat from a closet and put it on.

Jesse had picked up his own sweated Stetson. He was turning to the door when the doctor stopped him.

"Just a minute, Craven!" His voice was crisp and it brought Jesse's head around in surprise. "It's a long ride up to the bench. I'll go, but on one condition. You stay here!"

Jesse blinked. "Stay here?" he echoed. "What do you mean?"

"I mean that you'd only be in my way! I can tell when a man's on the edge of exhaustion. I'll get up there and do my job in quicker time if I don't have you to worry about. And you know there's not a thing in the world you can do to help Billy."

Jesse answered stubbornly, "My place is with my folks, a time like this. Ma'll need me."

"If you knew just how you look right now, you wouldn't want her to see you! You'd scare her to death!" And as though the argument had been settled, Talbot moved past Jesse and, at the door, took the knob. "I'll be back when I can; I'll tell you everything there is to know. Meanwhile, my cot's in the next room. You're welcome to use it if you want."

The door slammed before Jesse could do more than open his mouth to protest. He gaped at it in baffled resentment, hearing the echoes chase themselves down the corridor and then Paul Talbot's quick, brisk tread moving away. As silence returned he lifted a hand and worked stubby fingers through his untrimmed brown hair. He looked at the hat in his other hand; then, with a beaten shrug, turned back and dropped it again onto the chair where he had got it.

Doc, he had to admit, possessed an uncanny understanding. He knew when a man had reached the end of his tether—when he had spent all his reserves of strength. Jesse felt as though he had carried his family's burdens alone about as far as he could manage; it was a deep relief to be able to shift them, for a little while at least, to another's capable shoulders.

Reaching for the bottle and glass, he told himself he'd done all he could these past twenty-four hours. He'd brought back Ellie's bridegroom, he'd braved Mathison and the Spade Bit owner's gunman. He'd even killed a man. The help they needed now for Billy was not a kind he could give.

Now the whole thing was up to Doc.

Chapter Eleven

As the bedroom door opened, Ellie Craven, sewing by the window, looked up, and her mother quickly straightened from shaking down the cook stove. Both women waited in silence as Paul Talbot came out, carefully closing the door. He looked from one to the other and said, in tired satisfaction, "The boy's sleeping. He'll be all right."

Ellie laid down her work, hands suddenly trembling. Her mother, not speaking, took a battered tin basin from its nail, poured hot water from the kettle and placed it, with soap and towel, on the table. Talbot thanked her with a nod.

"It's nothing serious," he went on, as he washed and dried his hands. "The bullet hit a rib and followed it around. There was some loss of blood and the rib is cracked, but the wound itself shouldn't give too much trouble. Just keep him quiet until the rib has a chance to mend."

"You've taken a good-sized load off our minds," the older woman admitted, rubbing the palms of her hands across her apron. "We didn't know what to think. Bob and Homer are out at the barn," she added. "Ellie, you give Doctor Talbot some coffee while I go tell them."

The girl rose silently. The doctor pulled a chair back from the table and let himself into it, saying, "Thanks. I could use some coffee." The screen door slammed as Ma hurried out.

In silence, then, Talbot watched the girl moving about, getting down a cup for him and filling it. Her movements still held the inherent gracefulness of youth; she had not yet begun to appear heavy, though she showed her condition when she moved in silhouette across the sun-smeared window. Talbot hadn't failed to catch the dull gold sheen of the ring on her hand, that was new since his first visit here.

As the girl drew out a chair across the table, he observed her above the steaming rim of the cup. Her face appeared swollen, and there were the plain marks of weeping. The doctor frowned as he sipped his coffee. He was thinking of other small things he'd noticed.

He asked suddenly, "Do you know anything about the trouble at Mathison's, Ellie?"

She seemed at first not to hear his question. It was as though she brought her mind back from some far distance when, turning to him with a start, she answered, "No. No, they didn't tell me anything."

"I see." He drank the black coffee slowly. He knew he wasn't mistaken. There was something going on behind the surface—something he had first detected in Jesse, this afternoon. Since he liked Jesse—and, he realized suddenly, since he liked all this family—the hint of unexplained trouble worried him.

But then he reminded himself that it was none of his business, and he drained the cup and set it down. "I'll have to be getting back," he said. "And I was wanting to show your mother about changing the bandage."

"Why don't you show me?" the girl asked, and he looked at her in surprise. "I'm not afraid of blood."

He smiled a little at her indignant expression. "Just as you say, Ellie. Come into the other room."

Billy was sleeping peacefully, looking young and vulnerable and almost as white as the pillow under his head. Talbot drew down the sheet to reveal the neat bandage. He gave his instructions briefly, and the girl listened in silence, nodding to show that she understood.

"I'll do just as you told me, Doctor," she promised when he had finished.

He said, "I'm sure you'll make a fine nurse, Ellen." She would, too, he thought, suddenly more than ever aware of her as a person. He sensed that she had many of Jesse's qualities of strength and dependability.

Talbot knew Dade Haggis by sight; he looked at the ring on Ellie's finger now and he shook his head in disapproval. The girl was much too good for a worthless sort like that.

Hat and bag in hand, he exchanged a few more remarks and then stepped outside into the golden glow of late afternoon. Homer Craven watched silently as Talbot lashed his bag to the saddle strings and swung up. He blurted then, "I'm sure glad to know the kid will be all right, Doc. I'll tell you, we were scared!"

"I don't blame you."

"Guess we oughtn't to have gone down there, like that, but old Bob was pretty well worked up. We've had kind of a wild session around here—what with Ellie gettin' married this morning and Jesse killin' that guy at Pellman's—"

Talbot whipped a sharp look at him. "Yes?" he said, and thought, Was that it? But though he waited there were no details, and he didn't press for them. Still, he thought, perhaps he understood the sobering change that had puzzled and bothered him in Jesse Craven.

He said, briskly, "Be sure to let me know if Billy needs me again, but I don't think he will. Just keep him quiet, so he can build up the blood he lost—that's the main thing. I'll look at him again in a few days."

"Sure, Doc. Thanks again."

Talbot nodded and rode away into the pines.

Pete Horn said, "Who's the dude?"

"I dunno." Arch Suttle shrugged indifferently. "And care less! It's Craven I want to put my sights on. That's his folks' place, but I don't reckon he's there. Probably gone on below."

His companion scowled, narrowing now on the big man who still stood before the door. "A Craven's a Craven," he muttered, and the long-barreled gun slid out of his holster. Arch Suttle cursed and struck the arm aside.

"You damn fool!" he grunted. "Use your head or you'll bring the whole country down on us. Come on—let's go hunt up Dade."

Horn shot his partner an angry look, but he didn't rise to the argument. With a lift of his shoulders, he took the six-gun off cock and dropped it back into leather, afterward yanking the reins to turn his horse.

They had stopped just within the fringe of pines above the Craven place; they rode now up into the thicker growth, letting the clearing and the figure of Homer Craven drop from sight behind them, and swung directly east. The stain of the day's ride was on both of them, and on their gaunted horses. They hadn't exchanged a dozen words since leaving Pellman's, and they said little now as they threaded the scrub timber of this thin-soiled upland, keeping away from the scattered homesteads.

When at last they raised the Haggis place, they could see no sign of life. From the pigpen came the snaffling of the hogs, rooting in mud. The two horsemen drifted in and halted, and Arch Suttle rubbed a fist through the stubble on his long jaw. "Reckon he's around?"

Pete Horn was a stocky man, shorter then his companion. His head appeared to rest without a neck directly on sloping, heavy shoulders. His whole face seemed pushed together—the eyes small and squinting, the mouth crowded by chin and nose. On his cheeks were the many purple threads of broken blood vessels. He said, "He better be around! That's all I can say," and lifting his voice shouted Dade Haggis's name.

He called a second time before boots scraped inside the house and the blond man loomed up behind the screen door. Dade pushed it open and came out onto the stoop. He had a tin cup in his hand; he stared at his visitors as though in disbelief, and said, "I never thought I'd see you two again!"

They were piling out of saddle, moving stiffly and stretching soreness from their muscles. Arch Suttle demanded, "What are you drinkin'? I'm the thirstiest I ever been!"

Dade indicated the door behind him, with a backward jerk of the head. Suttle climbed the steps and went into the house. The one room was already shadowy. Seeing the jug of corn on the table, he went over and picked it up. He found a tin cup for himself, and stood looking around the squalid interior for a moment, before he discovered Dade's old woman.

She sat, with hands knotted in her lap, and rocked slowly back and forth on the edge of her chair, a twisted and complaining face lifted toward the window. Suttle stood and looked at her, but she continued her slow rocking motion, as though unaware anyone was in the room. He turned and walked out again, carrying jug and cup, and the screen jangled shut behind him.

Dade and Pete Horn had seated themselves on the edge of the stoop. "What's the matter with her?" Suttle demanded, easing down beside them.

"Aw hell!" grunted Dade. "Ain't nothin' suits her. She griped her head off when I pulled out yesterday, and now I'm back she don't like it any better."

Suttle had his drink poured. Pete Horn reached across

Dade and took the jug; having no cup, he levered it skillfully across a raised elbow and drank directly from the spout. He made a face as he set the jug down. "Don't know how you stomach the damned stuff!"

"If you don't like it, give it here," Dade grunted, and took the jug away from him and refilled his own cup. The liquor he had consumed was beginning to blur his speech, and put a glassy shine in his eyes.

"Don't sound very glad to see us," Arch Suttle said, "and after us ridin' all the way back here from Pellman's."

"I figured you'd be headin' the other direction and a hundred miles away by this time!"

"Scared of that Jesse Craven? That's what you mean, damn you?"

Dade shrugged, "You never acted too brave last night! You let him grab me and drag me out of there, and never lifted a hand!"

The lantern-jawed man slid his eyes away from the accusing stare Dade put on him. "He took us unawares," he admitted, "killing Bragg Novak the way he did."

Pete Horn said savagely, "That's the reason we come back. There's gonna be a settlement for Bragg. We're gonna get the bastard."

"You'll have to beat me to him," Dade warned, and drained his tin cup, afterward wiping a sleeve across his chin.

In the silence that fell on them, broken only by the gurgle of yellow whisky as Suttle filled his cup again out of the jug, the old woman's voice reached them from within the house: "Dade? Dade, honey?" Her son made an impatient face, not answering, and the querulous voice fell silent.

After a moment, suddenly reminded of something, Arch Suttle demanded, "Where's the bride? Did you go and make an honest woman out of her, like you was supposed to?"

Haggis gave him a snarling look. "Aw, lay off!"

"Maybe she wouldn't have him," Pete Horn suggested, his little eyes disappearing in a grin.

"Like hell! She tried to follow me home, but I sent her packin'. I want nothin' to do with no Craven trash."

"What do you aim to do now, Haggis? You ain't just gonna sit around in this dump. Let's find that cousin of yours and finish him, if that's what you want, and then make tracks for Silver Lode. Man, there's big money waiting!"

"Let it wait!"

Something in Dade's tone made the pair turn and look at him. His eyes had taken on a kind of wolfish intensity, suddenly, burning with the new thought that had been kindled in them. He said, "There's pretty big money right here!"

"Where?" demanded Suttle, looking around at the squalor of the Haggis place—the crude house and barn, the piles of junk, the scatter of empty tins with their torn labels. Dade made an impatient gesture.

"Down below," he answered. "Down in the valley, where my fine cousin Jesse sets such a store to bein' somebody important. He's always saying I make it hard for him—I give the whole bench a bad name!" All at once Dade was laughing, silently, his shoulders shaking.

Pete Horn said in exasperation, "What's so funny?"

"Why, you showin' up has put a different idea in my skull—something better'n just killing the bastard. We can finish him for good, and all the rest of the damn Cravens. And when we leave we'll have a stake in our pockets for when we hit Silver Lode!"

"Let's hear it, then. What's on your mind?"

"It'll need a couple more men. Do you know where we can get 'em?"

"Pellman will know—if your idea amounts to anything. Tell us what you're cooking up."

Dade held out his hand. "Pass the jug. . . ."

The hall door opening was the thing that roused Jesse. He lay in semidarkness, only half awake and not certain where he was, lost in the confusion that often attends returning consciousness. He heard footsteps in the outer office, and then the scrape of a match. As the lamp chimney clinked into place, a yellow glow seeped into this adjoining room and in one swoop of recognition everything came clear. Jesse groaned, a sound of self-disgust, and levered himself to a sitting position on the cot in the doctor's bedroom.

He was fully dressed, even to his boots—just as he had, unthinkingly, thrown himself down. One spur rowel rang, and at once he heard Talbot's question: "That you, Jesse?"

"Yeah, it's me."

He sat for a moment shaking his head to clear it, scrubbing a hand through tousled hair and across the back of his neck. Then he came up to his feet and walked into the office, as unsteady as if he were suffering from a real hangover and not from exhaustion.

A steely glow still remained in the sky outside the window, but lighting the lamp had changed the buildings across the street into massed silhouettes. Paul turned from hanging up his hat. He said, "You took my advice and had some rest. Good!"

"It isn't that good," said Jesse. "I have no business wasting a whole day! George Rickart will wonder where I've been, and I can't blame him. . . ." Then his eye lit on the bag beside the lamp; with a sudden shock he remembered. He looked up quickly. "What did you find out, Doc? How is he?"

"Billy?" The other nodded. He looked tired himself, grimed with the dust of the trail down from the bench. "The boy's going to be all right. Don't worry about him."

A dam of tension broke, and a great, weakening sense of relief flooded through Jesse. He laid a hand against the edge of the desktop. "It's a load off my mind," he said gruffly.

"A cracked rib and some blood lost. That's the extent of it. Their real problem is going to be keeping him in bed."

Jesse let his chest swell, in the first free breath he'd drawn since that horrible moment when the messenger arrived at Clevenger's. His thoughts moving on then to further problems, he demanded, "Did you hear any more details about the shooting?"

Talbot shook his head "I heard very little. From what your father said I gather that the bull was shot some time this morning, on his home pasture. At least, he was fresh slaughtered when they found him. A rifle bullet."

"This morning?" Jesse scowled at the lamp. Suddenly his head jerked, to a jarring thought: Dade Haggis, most likely riding that way to reach his mother's place, a carbine in his saddle boot, hatred of the Cravens rankling. The image grew clearer the longer he held it, and he was aware of the tightening of muscle that drew up his right fist into a knot. He murmured, "If I had any reason to think, for even a minute—"

"What?" the doctor prompted.

He shook his head, and forced the tension from him. "Nothing," he muttered, his tone changing. "Just talking in my sleep!" He stepped over and got his Stetson off the chair seat. "Well, Doc, thanks for everything!"

The other's voice stopped him before he quite reached the door. "Can you spare a minute? Of course, I don't want to speak out of turn."

Turning, Jesse gave him a puzzled look, but he shook his head and said with real feeling, "That's one thing you couldn't do, Doc!"

"I'm not so sure. This is about the shooting at Pellman's."

At once a coldness touched Jesse; reserve settled on him, like a mask. "Oh?"

"You see now what I meant about speaking out of turn." As Jesse stood waiting, answering nothing, Talbot came around the desk and seated himself on one corner of it. "I happened to hear it mentioned," he said, gently. "I thought you just might feel like talking about it. I've had a feeling something was bothering you—and you don't really strike me as the sort who could kill a man and shrug it off!"

"Nothing much gets by you, does it," said Jesse, when a long moment had dragged itself out. "I suppose you even knew all along that my sister wasn't married!"

Talbot made a small gesture. "I suppose I did—if it matters. Didn't I see a ring on her finger, this morning?"

"That's right. The man who done it to her—that worthless cousin of ours, Dade Haggis—he tried to pull his freight without making the thing good. But Billy and me trailed him to Pellman's and brought him back."

"Are you sure it was the right thing to do?"

To that, Jesse could only lift a blank, uncomprehending stare. "The right thing? I don't reckon I know what you mean!"

"I mean that your sister's a fine girl. It seems a shame for her to be tied to a creature like Haggis."

"You don't think we like the idea?" the other exclaimed scowling. "Good Lord, Doc! Under the circumstances, there was nothin' else we could do!"

Talbot shook his head. "I'm not sure I agree with that. There're worse things in the world than having an illegitimate child. Ruining Ellie's life, for instance, by marrying her to a man who wasn't worthy of her."

For just a moment Jesse hesitated, remembering the thoughts that had hit him when he rode to the Haggis place looking for Dade—disquieting thoughts of little Ellie condemned to spend the rest of her life toiling for that slovenly family, her child growing up to be one of the Haggis tribe.

But then he shook his head, deep-grained moral prejudices closing in on the startling idea this outsider seemed to be suggesting. "Maybe they look at things different where you come from, Doc," he said, stiffly. "But we're plain sort of folks here and we got our notions of what's right and wrong. Anyway, Ellie wanted the marriage. She thinks she loves the skunk!"

If the doctor seemed a little disappointed, he merely inclined his head. "Then there's nothing for us to argue about," he conceded. "So you rode to Pellman's? And killed a man there?"

Jesse had almost forgotten how their talk had started. The blunt question jarred him back onto the track of the conversation, the words stinging like a lash. "It was nothing I could help," he insisted. "The other guy forced me to it. He shot first, and he meant it for keeps. That's the Lord's truth, Doc!"

He realized suddenly that his voice had risen louder than he intended. The doctor's eyes were studying him, coolly; they rested on Jesse's face with a sympathetic regard that still had the power of working behind the defensive shield he'd reared, and reading what they found there. Talbot asked, in a quiet voice, "You'd never killed anyone before?"

"No."

"Yet I've noticed there's a general impression around here that life on the bench tends to get pretty violent."

"Not killing violent! Sure, we fight rough, sometimes, no holds barred. Once in a while when the whisky's passed around too often, there's a few might even drag a knife. But I'm no murderer, Doc! I—I wouldn't want to get to be like Roy Shull—able to gun a man down without even battin' an eye!"

Talbot came off the edge of the desk. He placed a hand briefly on Jesse's shoulder. He said quietly, "I doubt that you ever need let that worry you! There are some people who need killing; the one you shot was probably that kind of man. Don't brood on it, Jesse!"

The other nodded, a choking warmth rising in him. It was strange how this man was able, just by listening and talking, to make himself seem so much older—to penetrate to the root of nameless things that were troubling you, and give you the mature advice you needed. Actually, Jesse knew that Talbot was only a few years his senior.

"Thanks, Doc," he said slowly. "I'll remember what you've said."

It was full dark, the last glimmer of afterglow faded out of the night sky and the stars a bright mesh overhead. Coming up from the corrals, Jesse heard the homely sounds of a ranch headquarters settling down after a long day's chores—voices ebbing and flowing in the bunkhouse, the creak of a screen door and slap of water as the old cook stepped out of the kitchen to empty his dishpan. Lights in the windows of the main house shone out upon the grass and the undersides of the poplar leaves, giving them a waxen look.

Blanche came to him, moving almost soundlessly across the gravel of the path. She wore something white and full-skirted, that trailed about her in a filmy nimbus; she had drawn a dark shawl about her shoulders, but above this her face was dimly white and her hair caught a gleam from the lamplit window. She came directly to Jesse, and she spoke his name anxiously and reached to place both hands upon his shoulders. "We've been worried," she exclaimed, tilting her face up to him. "You have no idea!"

"Worried? About me?"

She explained: "George sent a man to Clevenger's after that boy from town was here looking for you. We've heard all about the fight you had at Spade Bit."

He shrugged, conscious of the weight of her soft hands. "I'd hardly have called it a fight. A little difference between me and Shull was all, and soon over."

"But he's a dangerous man!" she cried, on an indrawn breath. "You might have been killed. You mustn't take such chances—for anything!"

He started to answer something trivial and reassuring; but the words were never spoken. For with a sudden movement she came against him, and her hands slid up to his neck. Perhaps with defenses dulled by fatigue, Jesse felt his arms take her into their hard circle.

Her body was as he had known it would be—firm,

strong, enticing. Her mouth came up against his. And when, hardly understanding the roused impulses that raced through him, Jesse returned the fierce pressure of the kiss, the woman's lips parted beneath his own.

A little shocked, and suddenly aware of himself and what he was doing, Jesse drew back against the pressure of her arms. Releasing her abruptly, he broke free. "Blanche—" he said, gruffly, but that was as much as he could say. His head jerked suddenly; she too must have heard the crunch of gravel under the slow stride of boots, for she whirled. And abruptly, she was gone, the dress a moving cloud of white against the darkness as she went toward the house.

Jesse stood with his arms at his sides, staring after her, still aware of the feel of her and the startling, probing intensity of that kiss—and his own stunned reaction to a thing which he knew would never have happened under ordinary circumstances. After that he had to turn and face George Rickart as the latter came, unhurriedly, toward him.

Rickart was finishing an after-dinner smoke, and the cherry brightness of the cigar's end flared against the planes of his face, hardening its weak lines and putting a shine across his eyes that made their expression impossible to read. Jesse waited, a little numbed, and wondering how much those eyes might have seen, just now.

But George Rickart gave no hint to warn him. He halted in front of Jesse and, standing with hands deep in pockets and that unreadable expression on his faintly visible features. He said, "You're back late."

The other nodded. "I know."

Rickart took the cigar from his mouth, looked at the fired end and then put it back again. "What about this run-in with Mathison?" he asked, bluntly.

"It wasn't Mathison, it was that gunhawk of his. Pa and the boys were down off the bench, thinking that Spade Bit had killed their bull. There were some hard words, and my kid brother Billy got shot. Not serious, according to the doctor."

Rickart wagged his head, slowly. "I gathered it was something along those lines. You think Mathison killed the bull?"

"No, I don't, really. And maybe I can't blame him for losing his temper—especially when Bob deliberately booted over a wagon and wrecked it. Still, it was no reason for that trigger-happy Shull to put a bullet into the youngster."

There was a moment before Rickart answered, and his voice was slow and thoughtful as though he were forming his words carefully, working something out in his mind.

"I'm inclined to agree with you, Jesse. About Shull, I mean. I can't understand why Lorn Mathison should think he has to bring a man like that in here, and pay him good wages just to wear that gun around! I don't like it."

Heavy humor twisted Jesse's mouth. "Maybe," he said dryly, "he thinks the folks on the bench are planning to ride down here and wipe out the whole valley!"

"That's nonsense, of course," snapped the other man, and he took the cigar and dropped it into the gravel at his feet, and ground it with a boot. But something touched Jesse with a cold finger, and made him think, aghast: why, he must half believe it!

Before he could do more than open his mouth, to stammer some astonished answer, Rickart said abruptly, "Good night, Jesse," and turned on his heel. He walked away, leaving his foreman staring after him. Jesse Craven could scarcely have been more perturbed had the man upbraided him for making love to his wife.

Chapter Twelve

Now THAT HE'D COMMITTED IT to action, this idea of his didn't look quite as good to Dade Haggis as when he was working it out over a jug of corn. He almost wished he had the jug with him. The very thought of whisky became at once a need for it that made him squirm in the saddle and run a fist across his mouth—a fist that trembled a little, he noticed disgustedly. His throat and mouth felt as though they were sealed tight by the thirst he couldn't do anything about; there was a leaden weight in his belly as though his very guts had turned to cold, wet dough. Waiting, or fear, could do that to a man.

But he told himself nothing was going to go wrong; and anyway, there could be no turning back. Already he was approaching the edge of town, and by the timetable he had set up he knew that the others would be moving into their places with their actions geared carefully to mesh with his own. The whole job, as he'd planned it, depended on each man being where he was supposed to be, at the right moment. Arch and Pete he knew he could depend on. He hoped he could say the same for the other two Jim Pellman had sent him.

Just before he took the turn onto Main, at the chief crossroads, he caught the rumble of timbers that told him someone was using the old covered bridge over Buel Creek. That should be Arch and the one called Sam Benteen, entering town on schedule from the direction of the stage road. And sure enough, when he came in sight of the bank they were just putting their horses to the tie pole there and swinging down, slapping trail dust from their clothes. They looked like travelers idly sizing up a town that meant nothing to them one way or another.

Two broncs already stood at the pole. That was the one bad feature of the scheme—bunching the horses. And yet, when the moment came that they wanted mounts they would need them all at once, and they couldn't run the risk of getting separated.

Benteen, tying, looked up and nodded as Dade reined in. "Dead town," he remarked.

"Everybody's on roundup," Dade said, dismounting. "Place like this one pulls into its hole when all the outfits are on the range."

"Is there such a thing as a bank?"

"You're starin' at it. Don't look much like one, I guess."

The stranger glanced dubiously at the old building, with its front of pressed tin meant to look like brick. He said gruffly, "Hope they got money enough to change a fifty."

This Benteen was a spare and wasted man, with some shabby echo of gentility about him that made it seem almost plausible he could be carrying large money—that was why he'd been cast for the role he had. Arch Suttle, working on a cigarette, followed him across the walk now to the bank's open door, while Dade took a moment tying his own horse.

He cast a hurried glance along the street. Like as not the little dialogue they'd staged had gone unnoticed; there didn't seem to be anyone in hearing distance. The sidewalks were empty, the doors and windows blank. Only one other hitching post was occupied, across the street in front of the mercantile; there, a saddle horse stood bearing Clevenger's C Cross brand. Dade gave it a look, then looked again, more sharply. For just a moment, a nagging worry assailed him—a possibility he hadn't taken into account, and one that might throw everything out should the breaks go that way.

But then he shrugged. Too late to think about it now! He turned, ducking under the rail, and started for the open door of the bank.

Benteen had disappeared inside, but Suttle had paused there to set a match to his smoke. Face ducked behind his palms, he did not look up or display any slightest sign of knowing Dade Haggis, as the latter stepped around him and entered. A last glance into the street showed that Pete Horn had left the Colorado Bar on schedule, and was moving at an unhurried gait to the lineup in front of the bank.

The Colorado Bar had lost its own hitching post one Saturday night when celebrating cowboys had roped and pulled it out of the ground. Thus, there was nothing suspicious in that extra horse tied at the bank's rack, nothing to hint that Pete was moving into position to act as lookout man and have the mounts ready.

It was stuffy and breathless inside, with the morning sun smearing a dazzle across eastward-facing plate glass. Walking in, Dade gave the place a quick survey. In the middle of the room a customer stood at the writing desk, filling out a check. The pebbled-glass door of the banker's office was closed and on a bench near it a couple of men were waiting. One was a two-bit rancher from down the valley; the other was Lew Murphy, the second of the two recruits sent him by Pellman.

Murphy was a man of Roy Shull's stripe, though you had to see his eyes to realize it; it was somehow difficult to think of anyone with such a red, bulbous nose as being potentially dangerous. He looked harmless enough, sitting there on the mourner's bench outside Banker McCaig's office. His glance flickered as it crossed Dade's; He inclined his head in the smallest of nods.

At a desk in back of the railing a woman in a shirtwaist and ankle-length skirt was seated, clattering away at a typewriter. The teller, a thin-haired, nervous man, busied himself with paper work behind his grille; and there was Sam Benteen, already starting over to the window. Moving casually, Dade timed his own steps to arrive there just behind him.

Benteen had a greenback in his hand, which he shoved under the grille. "Change a fifty?"

"Certainly." Turning, automatically reaching for his money tray, the teller registered the size of the bill and swung back. "But that's only a—" The words died. Dade Haggis had stepped in as Benteen moved aside for him, and the teller looked squarely into the black bore of the gun Dade showed him through the bars.

He stared. He shifted his eyes to Dade's face, unable to speak for a moment. "This must be a joke, Haggis!" he stammered, and then quailed before the thing he read in the eyes above the gun.

"It ain't any joke!" Dade could understand the man's incredulity that anyone would dare to try a thing like this, by daylight and in a town where his face was known. What the teller failed to realize was that Dade Haggis didn't give a damn about being recognized. He was leaving this country and he aimed to give the fools something to remember him by.

With Benteen at his elbow to shield the gun, he knew that neither the woman nor the customers realized yet what was happening. He warned, in a voice that would reach no farther than the teller's ear: "Make any fuss and you'll find out how funny it is. Now, fill this!" With a deft movement he jerked an oat sack from beneath his coat. "Give me bills—no silver."

He saw what fear could do to a man, then. The other's face seemed to fall apart as courage died in him. Sweat shone across his scalp and his pink cheeks, and he wet his lips and reached to take the sack in a trembling hand.

Dade half turned for a searching look around. The typewriter still clacked away; the rancher on the waiting bench stared at the toes of his boots, unaware of anything but his own problems. But now the man at the writing desk laid aside the pen he had been using and, putting his checkbook away, turned toward the door. His look and Dade's crossed and held briefly. Dade Haggis didn't know his name, but thought he must be the new manager of the hotel here in Bueltown. A moment's uneasiness was quickly replaced by a feeling that the man sensed nothing wrong and that there was no danger in him.

But Arch Suttle was waiting at the door and Dade read the crawling suspicion in his eyes, as the man started that way. Dade, suddenly guessing his intention, had to check the cry of protest that nearly burst from him. After that it was too late, in any event; for Arch had lifted a hand to clamp the butt of his holstered gun, and abruptly the townsman halted.

Suttle's lips moved. Dade couldn't hear what he said, but at his command the other began to back slowly. He reached the big desk, sidled around it and placed his hands flat on the top, his eyes never leaving Suttle. Dade got a glimpse of his face, which was white with fear.

A single cold drop of sweat leaked down Dade's ribs. All at once he didn't know if he had the taste for a thing as chancy as this.

He snapped an order at the teller to hurry up his fumbling work of stuffing packets of green money into the sack. He was debating the risk of getting at the contents of the main vault as he sneaked another look at Arch Suttle, for the first time noticing how Arch was standing there directly in the doorway, his hand on his gun.

Didn't the fool realize that, from outside—

And then it happened.

Past Suttle's elbow, Dade saw the man who had come out of a store across the street and was heading this way, boots kicking up puffs of the loose red dirt. He was a small man, quick-moving; his hat shielded his face but Dade recognized him and was reminded of the single, saddled horse that had bothered him earlier. For now, in the middle of the street, Dave Clevenger suddenly halted. He was staring hard at Arch Suttle. Presently he turned his head and Dade knew he must also have discovered Pete Horn, waiting at the tie rack. And Dade's breath caught tight.

Clevenger wasn't wearing a gun. For the longest heart-stopping moment he merely stood where he was, not moving. Then all at once he jerked about in his tracks and had broken into a run, and as he went he shouted, "The bank! My God, they're holding up the bank!"

That was all it took to blow the lid off.

Horrified, Dade could only stand and watch Arch Suttle whirl around, heard his cry of rage as he brought up his gun. He saw Arch deliberately draw a bead on the running man, and fire. Clevenger had almost gained the opposite walk when the bullet stopped him. His body arched to the jar of the lead, his head flew back. One hand gropped blindly toward the place between his shoulders where the lead had gone in, before he was hurled forcibly to his knees and then down upon his face, to lie twisting feebly in the dirt of the street.

The gun's roar drowned the yell that tore from Dade—too late; but it had been too late from the moment Clevenger laid eyes on Arch, and on Pete waiting with the horses. He couldn't have failed to recognize the two of them, after the encounter Dade had heard about at Mule Ear Pass. He would have known for sure that such a man as Arch Suttle had no business standing in the door of the bank, especially with his hand on that damned gun.

The woman at the typewriter screamed, a sound that rasped the length of Dade's spine. At his elbow, he saw Benteen pulling a gun to cover the man at the writing desk, and Lew Murphy was lunging to his feet, likewise drawing. Then a movement in the teller's cage grabbed at Dade's dazed senses, and he whirled so violently that his gun struck a bar of the grille with a clanging impact that almost jarred the weapon from his hand.

Despite his terror, the teller had been fast to move when he saw a chance. His hand was coming away from the drawer he'd managed to open, blue gunmetal gleaming. An animal grunt broke out of Dade as, in a blind frenzy, he fired.

At that range he couldn't have missed. His bullet drove the man back, and he dropped gun and oat sack as he fell. Helpless, Dade watched the greenbacks spill and scatter. In a last desperate grab he tried at least to save the silver tray, but the bars prevented him reaching it, and a bright cascade of coins followed the teller to the floor.

At the door, Arch Suttle yelled hoarsely, "Damn it, let's get out of this!"

The crash of guns had already shocked the whole town awake with incredible suddenness. Dade was aware of voices yelling, and right in his ear the woman was screaming her head off, maddeningly. As he swung around, almost at the point of putting a bullet into her to shut her up, he had a glimpse of the bank president's door swinging open and McCaig's head framed in it. One look and the man ducked back, slamming the door shut again; but Lew Murphy was right after him. A single sweep of Murphy's gunbarrel splintered the pebbled glass. "Come out here!" he shouted, and grabbing the banker, yanked him through the jagged opening and hurled him to the floor, to join his terrified customers.

Dade Haggis looked again at the one he'd shot, a limp figure lying in a welter of silver and greenbacks. To get at the money, a man would have to circle the counter, go through a swinging gate—There wasn't time. For Arch Suttle was shooting again, at some target in the street. Now other guns were answering, and a hand grabbed Dade's elbow, and Sam Benteen shouted, "Come on!"

Empty-handed, cursing, and with fear a sickness in his belly, Dade turned and followed him out of the building at a run.

The street was utter confusion. Clevenger lay where he'd fallen. Nearer, at the hitch rack, Pete Horn sprawled —it didn't take a closer look to know Pete was dead. The horses were pitching and squealing in fright. And as they came pouring from the bank, Dade and his men ran into a hail of trouble.

Three or four townsmen had found weapons and the nerve to use them. Hugging the shelter of doorways and arcade posts, they'd already accounted for one of the gang. Now a bullet screamed past Dade's ear and he yelled something and threw off a shot, forcing some resident of Bueltown to duck for cover. He'd made it to the hitching post by that time and he ducked under, slashing at the reins of his sorrel to jerk them free. He reached for a leather with the same hand that held his gun, and almost lost them both. Terrified by gunfire, the sorrel smelled the fear on its owner and tried to shy away, but Dade pulled it down and threw himself at the saddle.

As he scrambled up, he saw Murphy leap to the cross bar and from there launch himself directly onto the back of a horse. Arch Suttle was trying to get his own bronc quieted enough to find the stirrup when the animal suddenly screamed and collapsed as a bullet struck it in the head. Arch didn't hesitate. He turned and flung himself at the roan that had belonged to Pete Horn; Pete wouldn't be needing it.

Then the four that were left had found saddles and were pulling away from the rack. "Follow me!" screamed Dade, swinging an arm. There was only one way for them now—the east trail, to the bench and the hills. He knew those uplands as well as anyone. The job he planned had turned out a failure; but now that it was a matter of fleeing for their lives, he challenged any man or any posse to cut the trail that he would lay.

A gun went off, almost in his face. The bullet sliced across his forearm like a knife blade, a mere scratch but startling in its burning fierceness. He looked ahead and saw the one who'd nearly got him—a hatless figure running out into the street for a second, better try. There wasn't time to shoot. A yank of the reins pulled the sorrel off course, sent it lunging straight at the man.

He stood his ground for just a second and then, losing nerve, hurled himself out of danger. Plankings thundered as the horse went up onto the sidewalk. Dade ducked his head under the arcade roof, giving the reins another pull, and made a short turn around the end of the corner building and thence down off the sidewalk again, into the farther cross street. He had to wait a second, then, for his companions to make the corner and catch up with him; they came, with Arch Suttle in the lead.

"How much did you get?" Arch yelled as they pulled abreast.

Dade shook his head, and other began to curse, his face thunderous. "Pete dead, and me with a smashed leg and a boot fillin' with blood!" Dade saw the red-soaked leg. Suttle went on, raging at him. "You and your damn big ideas—"

"Don't blame me! It was that Clevenger, seeing you and givin' the alarm."

"I hope I finished him!" His voice was tight with the pain of his leg.

Back on the other street, a hullabaloo was rising. Dade Haggis said curtly, "Save your breath, and let's get the hell out of this town while there's time."

He was already roweling the sorrel hard. It lunged ahead and he did not again look back; but he knew the other three were close behind as he headed for the open, and the trail that promised safety.

The rangeland grapevine was efficient. Paul Talbot never knew just how the word got carried so fast and so far, yet it seemed no time at all before the whole reach of this Buel Creek country knew about the trouble in town. By the time he had finished working on Dave Clevenger and felt it was safe to leave him alone and hurry across from his office to the bank, the street outside was already filling with men and horses, and with a boiling excitement.

He saw Lorn Mathison and Shull, and other Spade Bit men; George Rickart and Tom Nealy from Broad R; perhaps a dozen more representatives from the other ranches of the basin—and more were coming. Mathison caught sight of the doctor the moment he stepped onto the sidewalk. The rancher rode directly over through the mill of horses and leaning from saddle demanded harshly, "Doc! What about Clevenger?"

Talbot had allowed no one inside the office to bother him while he did his work on the injured man. He shook his head as they crowded in on him now. "I've done all I could. The bullet missed his lungs, but it ranged down through his body and I'm afraid there's internal bleeding. The shock itself was enough to kill a man."

He didn't know when he had seen such grim intensity in any face as there was now in Lorn Mathison's. The Spade Bit owner struck his saddle horn again and again with a tight-knuckled fist, and the eyes above his gaunt cheeks held fierce coals. He said tightly, "So this is what comes of letting mongrels like those run wild, up there on the bench! Dave Clevenger—the man who told me I was wrong about them and almost made me believe it! And now they've murdered him."

"Not yet. He may not die," the doctor reminded him, not liking the man's tone or the way his talk was reflected in the other faces.

Someone asked, "How bad hurt is Ed Ingram?" Ingram was the bank teller.

"His wound isn't too serious—Dade Haggis shot high. I had to let him wait until I'd tended to Clevenger. I'm on my way over there now."

"Here's Dave's girl," a voice called out, and at once the crowd fell silent and parted to make room.

The shiny black buggy was dust-filmed, the matched team glistening with sweat. One of the C Cross hands was managing the horses and Catherine sat beside him, looking pale and stricken; no need to ask if she had heard the news. Talbot stepped quickly to offer her a hand, and her fingers were ice-cold as she let him help her down to the sidewalk. She looked at him with eyes that were dulled by shock. "Where—is he?"

"Upstairs," Talbot answered. "Resting. Go right up—or do you want me to come with you?"

She shook her head. "No. No," she repeated in a

stronger voice. "I'm all right. You go ahead with whatever you have to do."

"I'll be back directly," he promised. "I'm glad you're here. It will be better if he isn't left alone. I'll be across the street at the bank, in case you need me."

"Thank you."

They all watched her enter the building and start to climb the stairs. Mathison said, in a voice that shook with fury: "To think that something like Dade Haggis could do this to the Clevengers!"

Doc Talbot looked at the rancher, about to remind him that it had been one of the others, and not Dade Haggis, who had fired the bullet. But he thought better of that pointless argument, and clamped his jaw shut.

Not liking at all the ominous note he heard in the hum of talk in this crowd, the doctor tightened his grip on the black bag he carried and crossed the street to the bank.

They had moved Ingram into the banker's office, and glass from the broken door crunched underfoot. The teller's wound was a clean hole in the shoulder; it was the shock of the heavy-caliber bullet at close range that had stunned him. Talbot cleared the spectators out and set to work binding up the man's wound.

As he was finishing McCaig came striding in, thoroughly rattled by his experience and chewing on a cold cigar in an effort to calm his nerves. He dropped into the chair behind his desk, and Talbot asked the banker, "You're sure they didn't get anything? You've made a count?"

McCaig shook his bullet head. "It isn't necessary. Miss Foley and two witnesses support Ingram's story. This man Haggis was the one who held a gun on the teller, while the others watched the doors and the customers. And Haggis was carrying no money when they were driven off."

"You've sent word to the sheriff's office, I suppose?"

"For what good it will do. It's a long way. I can't see him bothering about a robbery this far away from the county seat, especially when he finds out there wasn't any loss."

"To me, that seems an odd way to look at it! A law was broken, whether they took any money or not."

The banker gave him a look. He took the soggy cigar stub from his mouth to emphasize his next words. "You've still got some things to learn about this country, Doc—things that may shock you after the kind of world you came from! Out here we can't yell for help to the policeman on the corner. If you want law, you often have to make it yourself." He waved his arm toward the street. "Just what did you suppose those men out there were up to, anyway?"

"I know what I think they're up to," the doctor reretorted. "I don't call it law!" He snapped his bag shut, and left.

Sobered by his own thoughts, he had stepped out into the smash of the sun before he realized the noise out here had suddenly and strangely fallen off. He halted, looking quickly about. Saffron dust drifted; the noon sun glittered on the metal of saddle trappings, on guns and belt buckles and cartridges and spurs. The crowd had grown in these few minutes. New riders had joined them; even as Talbot watched, four more were coming up from the livery barn on rented animals. Townspeople lined the walks and filled doors and windows. Youngsters hung excitedly on the edges of the mob.

But for all the excitement there was stillness, now, as a single horseman approached along the street and drew in, with all the eyes of the crowd on him.

The man was Jesse Craven, and he bore that silent and hostile attention with a face that was set, Talbot thought, a little pale under its deep tan. From where he stood on the steps of the bank, only a few feet away, the doctor could see him plainly as Jesse raked a hard stare across the watching faces.

He found George Rickart among the others, then, and settled on him, twisting a little in the saddle to confront his boss. Jesse didn't speak loudly, but in the tense hush his words carried plainly. "Looks like I'm about the last to show up. I saw everybody pulling away from roundup and finally got curious as to what was going on—made the cook tell me. What is this, George? A secret?"

Rickart looked and sounded harshly uncomfortable. He ran a palm along his thigh and nodded, clearing his throat. "I'm afraid that's about it, Jesse. You weren't supposed to know."

"And why the hell not?"

Lorn Mathison answered him. The Spade Bit owner had dismounted; he stood beside his horse, one arm leaning against the saddle, and Roy Shull looming behind him. "Isn't it obvious?" he snapped, and brought Jesse's angry look around to him. "One of them that tried to rob the bank, and put a bullet in Dave Clevenger's back, was a man named Dade Haggis. He's kin of yours, I understand."

"What of it?" Jesse retorted, and a wild gleam flickered across his eyes. "Does that make me a bank robber?"

"And lying on a table at the undertaker's," the rancher went on, ignoring him, "is one of the cattle thieves we fought that day at the Mule Ears! I remember you trying to tell me there was no connection between your people and them that had been picking off my cattle. I guess now the truth begins to come out!"

"Hold on!" George Rickart exclaimed, as a stir went through the crowd. "It isn't anything like that, at all! This man can't be held accountable for everything that comes off the bench! As a matter of fact I gave orders that the news should be kept from you, Jesse, because I was hoping to spare your feelings. I was sure you wouldn't want to take part in this."

"What's more to the point," snapped Mathison, unrelenting, "was we knew damned well we didn't want you in it!"

The doctor could see the effort that Jesse Craven put on himself to control his temper. His face white with anger, Jesse refused to answer the arrogant Spade Bit rancher. Instead he turned away from him and threw a studying look across the group, all of them mounted and armed and waiting for the word that would set them loose on the mission they had gathered for.

He looked back at Rickart. "You're going up there?"

"Wherever the trail leads."

"And no one man," promised Shull, "is going to stop us!" It could have been coincidence that the shifting of positions in the saddle brought the muzzle of more than one rifle swinging in Jesse's direction. Shull's voice held open mockery as he added, "You see how it is, boy? Just keep out of our way!"

Jesse stared at him, and at the guns. Even from where he was standing, Paul Talbot could see the tightening of his facial muscles, the settling of his jaw. "Who's trying to stop you?" he snapped. "Go right ahead. But I'm coming, too!"

Talbot thought for certain, then, that there was going to be an explosion. Up to this moment he had believed he understood these people; had seen them as little different from others he'd known. But Howard McCaig had been right; in the quietest of these men there was a latent possibility of violence, and he was seeing it exposed now.

The break did not occur. Lorn Mathison gave an angry jerk of his head. "The hell with this," he said, and swung his gaunt length into the saddle. Lifting the reins high, he shouted, "We're losing time. Let's move!"

His piebald gelding squealed and leaped ahead; needing only a leader, the whole pack of riders responded. Boots kicked at dusty flanks. A mount neighed, trying to rear, but was cursed and brought under the bit. After that the whole mass of men and animals was flowing away up the long street in a tide of raised dust.

Paul Talbot saw Jesse hesitate for just a moment, letting the rush of riders go past him, saw him twist in the saddle, sending an anxious glance up toward the window of the doctor's office. Talbot knew he must have heard of Dave Clevenger's injury and was anxious to learn how Dave was faring; but another and stronger duty pulled at him. Before the doctor could do more than take a couple of strides forward, Jesse whirled his horse.

Talbot called after him but his voice was lost. And he halted, with both hands upon a hitching rail, to watch Jesse Craven spur after the other riders.

The hammer of hoofs battered itself against the false fronts; dust hung in the air and began to settle. The cavalcade was already shaking down into a steady, purposeful rhythm as it flashed from sight around a corner, taking the bench trail.

Chapter Thirteen

BY SOME MAGIC old Bob and the boys generally seemed to know without being told when dinner was ready. They came tramping in now from the barn just as Ellie finished setting out the last cracked plate and bent-tined fork, and amid loud talk took their places around the oilcloth-covered table—three big men smelling of horses and hay and sweat, Billy still wearing a bandage over his healing chest wound but not letting it interfere much with his normal activities.

Bob made a face at the bowl of boiled greens, but he helped himself generously and passed it on to his sons. Maud Craven was at the stove turning over the last of the steaks with a great popping and sizzling. As Ellie came with a steaming platter of meat, Bob leaned back in his chair and gave the girl a critical survey. He said, gruffly, "Daughter, how do you feel?"

"Me?" Ellie managed a smile. "Why—fine, Pa."

"You look a little peaked."

"Well, mercy," Ma shot back. "How would you expect her to feel?" She turned from her stove long enough to lay a hand on Ellie's shoulder. "You set down now. I can finish up here."

Ellie said, "I don't reckon I'm real hungry."

"You got to eat—for the baby."

Bob's grunt was sour. "That's right. Give him every break. God knows the odds are against him, with Dade Haggis for—" His head jerked up, his jaw stilled on a cheekful of fried beef. "Speak of the devil!" he grunted thickly, and his knife and fork clattered into the plate as he pushed back his chair.

The rest turned to follow his stare, through the window. Against a background of red pine trunks and sun-shimmering needles, two riders were coming down the trail into the hollow. They rode slowly, to accomodate the efforts of one of the men to stay on his horse. He reeled in the saddle, hanging to the horn and behaving as though he might be out of his head with agony. And a look at his blood-drenched left leg was enough to tell why.

But there was no sympathy in Bob Craven's stern face as he strode to the door, pausing to lift an old Henry rifle down from the pegs where it rested. He hooked it across a bent elbow, pushed the screen door open and stepped outside. Boots spread, he stood and shouted at the approaching horsemen: "You, Dade Haggis! Get away from here!"

Dade had been turned in the saddle, looking behind him as though wary of his backtrail. He whipped around, and at the vehemence in Bob's words he shortened rein, almost halting. But he shook his head doggedly, and he called back, "We're comin' in!"

With an expert movement old Bob flipped the Henry off his arm, worked the lever and slammed it into place, and threw the stock against his slabby thigh. "I told you once," he shouted, "never to stick your face around here again!" And he fired.

He aimed at the ground, a foot ahead of Dade's sorrel; dirt geysered and the animal tossed its head, promptly backing away a couple of steps. Arch Suttle's horse bucked and its loose-sitting rider almost went off the saddle before Dade could put out a hand to steady him.

"Damn you," he yelled, through the dying echoes of the shot. "My friend's hurt bad. You gonna just let him die?"

"If he's a friend of yours, he probably deserves to!"

But Maud was at her husband's side now, and she laid a hand on his wrist. "He's a human being," she said, quietly. To Dade Haggis she called, "Bring him in. I'll see what I can do."

Bob had an expression like thunder, but he slowly grounded his rifle butt and stepped aside. He waited like that in the hot noon sun, unyielding, as the horses lagged forward. Both mounts were lathered and dust-marked; they had been used hard, and so had the riders.

Dade's shirt sleeve was ripped and there was dried blood on it. They came to a halt. At a word from Maud, Homer and Billy crowded out past their father to help ease Arch Suttle from his horse. The hurt man cursed them viciously but they got him down, and with one of his arms across each of their shoulders, helped him inside.

Dade Haggis didn't dismount. Instead, throwing another look behind him at the trail, he caught up the reins of the other horse and turned toward the pines. He rode out of sight into the timber, to appear again after a moment on foot. Bob stood and watched him come close, slapping dust from his clothing with his hat. But at the door the old man stopped him.

"That's a bullet wound he's got!" he grunted, his eyes locked with Dade's. "And your arm has blood on it. What are you two running from? Why did you hide them horses? What devilment you been up to?"

Dade met his stare, insolently. "Go to hell!" he grunted, and shouldered past and into the house.

They had let Arch Suttle down onto a chair, where Billy stood holding him while Homer and his mother worked to tear away his bloodsoaked jeans. The boot was filled with blood, and that had to be cut free. Dade said, "What do you think?"

"Pretty bad shot up," Maud answered. On her knees,

she looked around. "Ellie," she ordered crisply, "you better not watch this!" But it wasn't sight of the blood that had turned Ellie's face white, and made her cling to the back of a chair to steady herself. She was looking at Dade, her eyes wide. When Dade returned the look his expression didn't soften, and his glance passed on. After that first moment he seemed unaware that his wife was there.

"The bullet's gonna have to come out," Maud Craven was saying. "Homer, you fetch the jug—let him have a drink first."

Bob, who had followed Dade into the house, said now, "Hell! Gimme that knife, and get out of the way. Boys, you hold him good and tight!" Swinging around, he straddled the hurt man's thigh and clamped the bloody leg against his chest. Knife poised, he threw Suttle a warning across his shoulder: "You kick me in the face, mister, and you'll wish you hadn't!"

Afterward, with the horrible twist of lead removed and the mangled wound washed with raw whisky and bound in clean rags, Bob finished drying his hands and turned to Dade Haggis. His manner was still hostile and unbending. "I'm still waitin' to hear what kind of a mess you've gone and got yourselves mixed up in. Whatever it is, we don't aim to get dragged into it. Understand?"

"You won't be," the yellow-haired man retorted. "We'll be off your necks in just a minute." His eyes strayed to the table, where platters of meat and vegetables were growing cold. "I'm starved. How about some grub?"

"Not at my table. Quicker you're out of here the better I'll like it!"

Dade shrugged, and looked at Arch Suttle. "You up to ridin'?"

"Give me a hand."

The pain of extracting the bullet and cleansing the wound had left him limp, but a couple of slugs of the potent Craven whisky seemed to have revived the man. On an empty stomach, it had likely hit him hard. His head lolled and, when Homer got a grip on his arm to help him up, he responded with the loose give of a man close to half drunk. "I'll fetch the horses," Dade said.

That was when Billy, at the door, cried out suddenly: "Hey! More riders, Pa—three of them." He added, in a voice gone tight: "It's that Shull, and a couple of Mathison's men—"

With a curse, Dade wheeled toward the door, grabbing at the gun in his belt holster. Before he could level it on the three riding unsuspectingly into the hollow, a heavy hand closed on the weapon and jerked it from his fingers.

"None of that, damn you!" gritted Homer, holding the gun. "Somebody better disarm the other one, just to be safe." Arch Suttle made no resistance as the six-gun was lifted from his own holster; he scarcely seemed to notice.

Dade said tightly, "That's a damn fool thing to do. When Shull finds us here—"

"So it's him that you're running from?" old Bob exclaimed. "What did you do to Spade Bit? Answer me!" Dade, though, had turned close-mouthed and sullen.

Homer said, "Pa! There's no time for this. Whatever they did, we can't turn 'em out for Shull to murder. Until we know what's going on, let's get the pair of 'em out of sight—quick!"

Old Bob looked around at his son, his anger dampened.

"Up there," Homer added, and pointed toward the loft ladder.

His father squinted at it dubiously and then at Arch Suttle, still groggy with pain. "He'll never make it!"

"Yes he will. Come on! Dade, give us a hand, damn you!"

A single word in his behalf was all Dade Haggis needed, and he moved quickly to obey while Bob seemed of a mind to follow his son's advice. It had to be done fast, because the riders were very close now, slowing to study the ground as though they might have found interesting sign there. But Arch Suttle appeared to understand the danger closing in on him, and he made an effort to help lift himself up the ladder, his hurt leg trailing.

Among them they got him through the manhole and into the loft; Homer, leaping down, saw the bloody boot and the basin and the remains of the rags they'd used to bandage him with. "Quick Ma!" he exclaimed. "Get rid of that stuff!" She hurried to take care of it as old Bob, snatching up his Henry, turned to the window and drew aside the scanty curtain.

One look and he was leveling for a bead on Roy Shull's chest, his intent plainly written in the grim lines of his face.

Ellie's hand caught at his arm. "Pa! No!" She couldn't budge him. Out there, Shull had reined in and was looking off toward the fringe of pine, and he made a motionless and perfect target.

Eyes squinting along the line of the sights, Bob said, implacably, "He tried to kill my boy! I'll never have another chance like this." Unmindful of her protests, his hand went white about the knuckles as it clamped the stock, finger beginning to take up the slack, the Henry's barrel rock-steady.

But then Homer's steadying voice seemed to reach him. "Pa, she's right and you know she is! It's murder! You kill one and you'll have to make it good and finish all three. And what have we got against the others? You can't just shoot 'em down!"

Slowly, very slowly, the rifle barrel sagged out of line. Old Bob lifted a hand, ran the knuckles over his mouth and across the scrape of his jowls. The rifle pointing at the floor now, he said heavily, "All right. I reckon I'll have to palaver with them."

The three had pulled up and Shull, after a searching look around, was starting to dismount when the screen door slapped shut behind Bob. Standing on the slab of spur-gouged pine in front of the door, the old man shouted, "Put your pants back in that saddle, mister! You got no business here at all."

Shull seemed to debate with himself, and then took the warning and settled again into leather. He looked at Bob, and the slant of the Henry. Behind Shull, the two Spade Bit hands were on a nervous tether, watching to see what Shull would do.

"Now, ride!" old Bob ordered, "while I'm in a mood to let you!"

Shull revealed no fear of the Henry, or of any other guns that might be trained on him from within the house. He raked Bob with his slow stare and a sneer warped his mouth. "What's graveling you? Still sore over what happened to your kid, that time? He's gonna have to learn better than to pull a gun on me!"

From beyond the door came Billy's angry voice: "Damn you, I never—" He was cut off, silenced probably by Homer.

"You can have just as much trouble as you ask for, old man," Shull continued, in the same tone. "Show some sense. Where are they?"

"Who?" grunted Bob.

"You know who! We trailed 'em pretty near this far, and one of them at least is bad shot up. You being kin to that Haggis—his father-in-law, according to what I heard—"

"You mean Dade?" Bob tried to make his voice sound surprised. "What's Dade been up to?"

Shull said, "You didn't know about him and four others trying to hold up the bank in town this morning?" He must have recognized the honest bewilderment of Bob's shocked look, for he went on, "Well, they sure as hell did! Didn't get away with nothin' and one of the bunch was killed; but the rest made it up here. And we're out to comb this bench until we hit sign of them!"

The puncher added, "If Dave Clevenger dies, it's gonna mean the rope."

"They shot Clevenger?"

Bob's expression was one of horror. The question died on his lips and he stood open-mouthed, working on words that refused to come. And in that moment, while the old man was plainly stunned and past moving quickly, Shull made his play.

A sudden stab of the spur, and the horse under Shull was lunging straight forward. Bob loosed a cry as he tried to step away, bringing up the Henry; but the logs of the house wall were behind him and next instant the sweaty shoulder of the horse rammed him hard. The solid wall of the house shook with the weight of the animal. Shull's left hand found the barrel of the Henry and a swift wrench plucked it from Bob's fingers, sent it end for end into the yard in a wheeling arc of sunlight. Shull's belt gun had left its holster, in the same flashing move; his horse, crowding old Bob, had all but knocked the wind and the sense out of the old man. Now Shull leaned over him and his gun's muzzle jabbed against his victim's neck.

"You in the house!" he shouted. "If you want him dead, go ahead and use that gun!"

Homer Craven was stopped in midstride toward the door. There was no underestimating his father's peril. He blinked at Shull and at the cocked gun waiting to tear old Bob's head off his body. His mouth opened and he swallowed; and then, automatically, he let his hand open and the heavy six-shooter fell.

Still not easing the threat of his own weapon, Shull glanced at one of his men and signaled him, with a nod toward the house. At once the puncher dismounted and, squeezing past the rump of Shull's horse, opened the door and walked in, gun ready. Old Bob had found his voice now; white and trembling, sweat filming stubbled cheeks, he glared up into Shull's face and began to curse.

The gunman looked at him. "All right, pop. Where's the ones we're lookin' for?"

"I don't know."

"Stop lying!" Quite deliberately, Shull struck with the barrel of the gun—a sideswiping blow, hard enough to daze a man. Slowly old Bob sagged down the wall and dropped to his knees; the gunman, swinging down, ordered gruffly, "Bring him inside." And as the second Spade Bit rider moved to do so, Shull entered the house.

He saw the closed doors to the two bedrooms and at once went and kicked them open, gun leveled. Finding no one in either room, he came scowling back to the center of the kitchen. "We know they were here," he said, in a voice that held ominous warning. "So somebody'd better talk up!"

Still he got no answer. In a hard silence he turned upon his heel, letting a glance probe each face in turn. He halted suddenly; Ellie Craven drew back a step, as the heavy stare came to rest on her.

The gunman's eyes sharpened. "You must be the gal Luke Wigfall told somebody they shotgunned Haggis into marrying!"

A couple of strides brought him to a stand over the girl. She had backed against the table with its ruin of an uneaten meal; halted there, she stared into his mocking eyes and her face was white but resolute.

"Pretty, huh?" murmured Shull, with a flicking glance at his men. "I always did like that color hair!"

The girl cringed away as his hand touched her head, fingering the copper curls that lay against it. All at once his hand was twisting tight in her hair, with a yank that pulled Ellie's head painfully back, a gasp breaking from her. "Your husband was here just a few minutes ago," the gunman said harshly. "Where is he now, damn you?"

"Shull," cried old Bob, in a voice that trembled. "You take your hands off my daughter, or by God—"

He didn't get to finish. For it was at this moment one of the Spade men happened to notice the ladder built into a corner of the room. His look followed it up to the dark square of the hole in the ceiling and he shouted, "Hey! What do you reckon is up there?" A grunt broke from Shull, as he jerked around. This was something he had missed.

Without hesitation he released Ellie and swung in that direction. A feral gleam of anticipation kindling in his eyes, Shull raised his gun. "Come on down," he ordered. There was no answer, not even the sound of a breath in the room. Tensed, the Cravens watched him walk slowly to the ladder, his gun ready. He lifted a boot and set it deliberately on the bottom rung.

Jesse Craven's voice demanded, sharply, "What do you think you're doing?"

For a frozen instant Shull didn't move, and then his whole body twisted. Jesse stood in the doorway, Tom Nealy at his elbow. No one had heard them ride in, or the screen pull open. Jesse's face was grimly set, the gun in his fist held squarely on the man by the ladder. Shull looked at his face, and then at the gun. And the muscles in his own jaw bunched.

"What does it look like I'm doing?" the gunman retorted. "I'm hunting a killer."

"Hunt all you want to—but not here! I can tell you right now, my folks wouldn't let such as that on the place! And the same goes for you!" Jesse added. "I'm giving you five seconds to put up that gun and get out!

"I mean it, Shull!" he warned when the other didn't move. "After what you did to my brother, I'd drop you where you stand! You better not tempt me."

Shull was beginning to breathe heavily. He flicked a look around and saw that his two men had already dumped their own weapons back into the holsters; Tom Nealy had slipped in behind Jesse and was watching both of them narrowly.

Color began to flood into Shull's face, staining it a congested, angry red. With a sudden savage thrust he rammed his gun home, but his hand hung just above the holster mouth, fingers flared above the jutting handle. "Put it away," he challenged, his eyes boring into Jesse. "Empty your hand and let's start from scratch! You and me have been building up to this. Why don't we finish it right now."

"I'm no gunfighter. I wouldn't stand a show facing it out with a man of your speed. And I won't be talked into committing suicide! Though maybe at that," Jesse added, his voice bleak, "I may have to try my luck some day, if you don't leave my folks alone. Now, you and this pair get the hell out of here!"

Given any sign of support, Shull might have resisted. But the Spade Bit men were cowhands, and probably not too happy about anything that had happened here, including his rough handling of the girl. He lifted his shoulders in a shrug, and looked around at the silent Cravens. "Nothin's settled," he warned them. "Those crooks were here, and I know it!" But then, with a jerk of the head for his men, he headed for the door. Jesse and his companion drew back to give the three of them room, and followed them outside to watch while they got reins and stirrups and swung into their saddles.

When they were gone, Jesse turned to his folks, who had piled out of the house after him, the men carrying the guns they had retrieved. His mother asked, "Is it true about Dade and the bank?"

Jesse nodded. "I'm afraid so. Dade's gone bronco, for sure. He isn't the one that shot Clevenger, but it's on his head just the same, and the whole basin's up in arms and looking for him. I know I don't have to tell you that if he should dare to show his face around here, under no circumstances are you to let him light!"

"Jesse—" She didn't finish whatever she'd been about to say. She glanced at Bob, out of the tail of her eye, and he was shaking his head. Tom Nealy stood only a couple of paces away, watching and listening. Maud Craven closed her mouth as Jesse went on.

"We'll have to ride. If you keep your eyes open I don't think Shull will have the nerve to bother you again." He nodded to his companion and started for his own horse; but then he turned back, and going to his sister he placed his hand for a moment on Ellie's shoulder. "I'm sorry, carrot top," he muttered. "Sorry as hell!"

He gave her shoulder a squeeze, and then strode to his horse. Bob and the others stood and watched in silence as the pair of riders took the trail into the pines and vanished in the wake of the men from Spade Bit.

It was Maud who spoke at last. "We should have told him!" she cried. "Jesse would have known what to do if we'd just told him."

"How could we?" Bob countered, scowling and fingering the side of his head where Shull's gun barrel had raised a painful lump. "With that other fellow listening to every word we said? Dade's no damn good, but for the sake of Ellie's child we can't see him hung for a bank robber!"

He swung about and threw an order at his waiting sons. "Homer," he ordered, sourly, "You and Billy fetch that pair down from the loft. Minute the coast is clear we kick 'em off the place—and let's hope to God we never lay eyes on either of 'em again!"

Ellie, her white face downcast and hands tight clenched, said nothing.

Chapter Fourteen

Roy Shull told his men, "First one of you lets loose a word of what happened back there is going to regret it. You understand me?"

The Spade Bit punchers exchanged a nervous look and nodded, recognizing the danger of this man. Shull let the pressure rest on them for a moment, studying them with his corrosive glance until he decided they could be counted on to keep their mouths shut.

He nodded, the matter settled, and roughening his voice he said, "All right! Now, go along—I want to ride by myself for awhile."

A hard amusement was in him as he pulled out of the trail and slanted up a long rise into cedar growth, leaving them behind. In the trees he reined in and looked back to see that they had taken their orders and were jogging away from him along the trail, lifting red dust for the wind to scatter. Shull clucked to his horse, and moved ahead on a circling course of his own.

The sun at midday held heat, but up here you could tell that summer was really over, for the wind that blew was the actual breath of fall. The sky held the hard blue of autumn; the aspens of the high timber slopes above the bench had turned and were splashes of yellow. Down in the basin, fall roundup had been under way now for almost a week, and sizable herds in the various basin brands would already have been collected on the holding grounds.

The excitement of the turning season, with its crispness that started the blood singing in a cowman's veins, meant nothing to a man like Shull; and yet the thoughts that had begun spinning in his mind brought their own heady excitement. He was in a pleased mood as he came down again through pine, riding cautiously now, and once more brought the Craven place into sight.

Only a few minutes had been lost. Sheltered by the trees, Shull watched the buildings briefly and then moved ahead, finally dismounting. It did not take him long to find what he was looking for; he had been quite certain there would be saddled horses here somewhere, waiting. The only question was, how many? But there were only two, which offered no problem. He tied his own horse back in some brush, and settled patiently to roll a cigarette which he put between his lips without lighting.

It was not long before he heard someone coming. He tossed the cigarette aside. His shoulder against a tree bole, motionless in its shadow, he saw Dade Haggis break into view and move quickly toward the horses. The blond man was alone, and he was scowling.

Shull watched him turn the stirrup to receive his boot. He said, pleasantly, "Going somewhere, Haggis?"

Breath gusted out of the man. He jerked around so sharply that his boot slipped on pine needles and he almost fell. He searched wildly for a second before he located Shull. When he saw who it was the blond man's face broke apart in a gape of horror, and he made an unwise grab for the six-gun in his holster.

Shull's arm seemed scarcely to move, but one instant his hand was empty and then there was the gleam of the blued gun barrel, pointing straight at the other. "Don't be a damn fool," he said, crisply, and Dade Haggis's movement froze suspended, uncompleted. His face shone from the sweat that had started out upon it.

"Where's the one belongs to the extra horse?" the gunman demanded. Still he got no answer, and he let irritation pucker his eyes and pull at the corners of his lips. "All right," he grunted. "Be stubborn!"

Dade said hoarsely, "You knew we was up in that loft?"

"Of course I did. I could tell from the way they all acted—they gave it clean away. Hadn't been for that cheeky cousin of yours—" He shrugged, letting his anger die. "Well, that's all right too, now that I've had time to think things over!"

In spite of his peril, there was something in the words

that made the prisoner ask, curiously, "What things?" But Shull didn't answer the question directly. Instead, he asked one of his own, as he looked thoughtfully at Haggis.

"Haggis, what sort of a man are you? Have you got any real guts in you? If I thought you had, we might be able to make a deal."

"A deal?" Dade's eyes darkened with bewilderment, but also with a beginning hope. "You mean me and you?"

"It could be. How many were with you in Bueltown this morning? Four?"

"Pete Horn was killed. That leaves only three."

Shull frowned. "Not enough!"

The other was beginning to forget his fear, now. "There's Jim Pellman," he suggested, eagerly. "He can always turn up a few, even on short notice. But it would have to be made worth his while."

"Don't worry about that!" grunted Shull. "It's a big idea I'm working on. Thousands in it for everybody!"

Dade Haggis could only stare. He touched his tongue to dry lips. "You—you're just makin' fun of me, ain't you?"

"Hell, no. I'm thinkin' of something that would make that bank job this morning look like piker stuff! And I'm willing to deal you in, Haggis, if you think you'd have what it takes to carry out your end."

Relief from the terror of a moment ago was mingled, in the blond man, with a newly kindled greed. He said, eagerly, "You could at least give me a chance!"

"Maybe I will, at that," said Shull, and on a sudden decision his gun slid back into its holster. "Only one thing stands in the way of what I have in mind, and I think I know how to take care of that!"

Yes, he was sure now, sure of every step in the program, the problem of disposing of Jesse Craven having found its solution in the minutes he'd stood here under the trees, waiting. He nodded in satisfaction and, watching the other carefully, made his announcement.

"I'm fed up with Mathison, is what it comes to. He's pulled his airs on me once too often! I been fed up a long time. And right now, Haggis, I'm thinkin' the time's come for me to sell him out."

That afternoon, with late sunlight just touching the highest leaves of the poplars with gold and the ranch yard itself in shadow, a council of the manhunters was held at

Broad R. Saddled horses, sweated from long hours of trail work, stood about the yard. Punchers talked and smoked along the porch rail and at the corral, and invaded the cook house for coffee and grub while they waited for their employers to finish their serious talking.

Nearly a dozen men crowded the living room. Shadows were piling in the corners but no one had thought to light a lamp, or build a fire in the fireplace against the chill that would be coming as night settled. George Rickart sprawled, slump-shouldered, in one of the big leather chairs; he had stripped his spurs, laying them on a scarred oak table, and he had his legs stretched out and was idly waggling his boots. Lorn Mathison stood before the cold fireplace. Jesse Craven, straddling a ladder chair with his arms folded across its back, listened to the talk and tried to ignore an occasional hostile look that came his way. What he couldn't ignore was the stony glance of Roy Shull.

Shull had come in just a few minutes earlier, his clothes stained with the red dust of the bench, and had taken a stand against the wall across the room from Jesse. The gunman's eyes bored at him. They seemed to hold speculation, as if he were biding his time, waiting for some propitious moment.

One of the ranchers, a cautious man named Stackpole, broke into the run of talk with a stated decision of his own. "Well, I can tell you this! If you're going to hunt any longer you'll have to count me out. This is the wrong time of year to pull my men off roundup and go chasing bank robbers. After all, it ain't as though there was any money gone."

Rickart looked up at him, scowling. "That's kind of shortsighted, isn't it? What about Dave Clevenger? You heard what Talbot's supposed to have said—that his chances were so slim they might as well put him in a wagon and haul him home, since he was set on it. Doc says he can die there as well as in town! If he dies won't that mean anything?"

"And there's more to it," another man spoke up. "Nothing like this has ever happened on Buel Creek, but you let one bunch get away with it and you'll be inviting somebody else to try. We've got to stretch some hemp, if we expect to set an example skunks of that stripe can understand!"

Stackpole appeared to waver, under these arguments. "I dunno," he muttered. "One of 'em was killed; that ought to do something to slow 'em down. Besides, who says it would ever happen again?"

"Why, the bench is still there, ain't it?" Roy Shull's words, flat and without emphasis, cut into the other voices. "What came off it once—"

He let it go unfinished, his eyes pulling back to Jesse Craven. Jesse had lunged to his feet, thrusting the chair aside. As he moved, his gun gear creaked, and the sound was loud in a room that seemed suddenly to be holding its breath.

"Jesse!" exclaimed George Rickart, sharply.

"I've been waiting for him or someone to say that," Jesse Craven stated, ignoring him. "Okay, let's have it out! Only one man in that whole crowd was from the bench, and you know it!"

Mathison said sharply, "We don't know it!"

"I do," Jesse retorted. "And I'm telling you! As for Dade Haggis, the man's a renegade—and the bench has no more use for that kind than anybody else. Not a family up there would take him in, after what he did today."

"No?" murmured Shull, and his eyelids drooped. "Do you think you're fooling anybody?"

It was too much. Shull's goading hadn't done the trick, up at his folks' place; but now a blazing fury seemed to explode in Jesse and, forgetful of the danger and even of the gun in his own holster he burst across the room, his hands reaching. At once the gunman was at a crouch, waiting for him, his right hand cocked and ready to draw.

But Lorn Mathison took a quick step and caught Jesse, hurling him back. Mathison was between him and the gunman then and he said sharply, "That's enough, Craven. Let's have no trouble out of you!"

"Me?" echoed Jesse. "Damn it, he's the one who—"

"I said that's enough! We know where your sympathies lie, I guess. By rights you have no business here at all."

"What do you mean by that?"

Mathison shrugged, while the rest of the room watched and waited. "Do I have to spell it out, Craven? You're the same outlaw breed as the rest of that shiftless bench crowd. To me it's no wonder we could hunt all day without finding any sign of the men we were looking for. Naturally, you'd see to that."

Jesse felt his nails grind into the palms of clenched fists. Through his teeth he said, "You'll take that back!" Despite the buzzing in his ears he knew Rickart was shouting his name, but it scarcely registered. Even the quarrel with Shull was forgotten. In that instant his whole attenion was focused on the gaunt-cheeked, arrogant face of the Spade Bit owner.

He heard himself saying, "You really think everyone on the bench is lower than dirt, don't you, Mathison? Tell me why. There was a few minutes, once, when I thought you might be almost human—that day at your place when my brother Billy got shot. I thought there was a chance you had some grain of sympathy in you, seeing that Billy was just a kid, and hurt. Looks like I was wrong! The truth is, you don't understand my people, and you don't want to."

Lorn Mathison said coldly, "You through talking?"

"Not quite. Roy Shull I can understand—but you! I've been trying to figure out why it is you've worked so hard, making trouble for those folks up there. You know the conclusion I've come to? I think it might be that you're jealous!"

"Jealous?" The grooved cheeks settled into an incredulous scowl. "Of that trash?"

"Why not? They ain't got much—but they got a sight more than you, for all your grass and your blooded stock and the men who kowtow to you and draw your gun wages! What are you, anyway?" he went on recklessly. "Just a surly bachelor with the blood dried up in you, all burned out with ambitions that don't net you a minute's pleasure! I'm thinkin' you took the wrong road somewhere, and you know it. And now when it's too late for you, my people keep reminding you of some of the things you missed. That must be why you hate 'em!"

The rancher was staring at him, the color whipped high in his sunken cheeks and his eyes blazing. He found his voice now and he cried, "I'll listen to no more of this!"

"Might be good for you, if you did," said Blanche Rickart.

Every head turned. She had come through an inner door, unnoticed, as all these men listened in dumbfounded silence to the scene between Jesse and Mathison. She leaned there now, a hand on her hip; fading light from a west window touched her and turned her yellow hair to a gleaming crown of spun gold. George Rickart, on his feet now, told her hoarsely, "You'd better stay out of this!"

"Why?" She tossed her gleaming head. "Jesse's been telling the man the truth about himself; and for your own good, George, you ought to make him see it. Do you want to be as big a fool as he is—perhaps even let him drag you into a full-scale war with those bench people?"

Mathison, staring at her, said in a voice gone suddenly too quiet, "So I'm a fool, too!" He seemed to have grown conscious, all at once, of these others watching him, and his voice trembled. "I don't have to take that!"

"You don't, for a fact!" Roy Shull told him, in a tone of silky satisfaction. "Not from these two! Have you forgotten, boss, what we saw that day on the town trail?"

His boss turned and looked at him blankly for a minute, and then understanding darkened his eyes. George Rickart followed the shift of his glance; he swung his head from Jesse to his wife, and back again to Mathison.

"What's he hinting at?" Rickart demanded. Suddenly his face lost color and there was the first revealing flutter of tight cheek muscles. He blurted hoarsely, "It isn't true!"

"Oh, but it is," Mathison said. "We were both there, George. We heard a bronc and rode to have a look. I could hardly believe it myself when we saw—"

"Saw what?" cried Blanche. "Say it, and he'll know you're lying!"

But Jesse, reading her husband's congested face, knew it was already too late. "No, Blanche!" he groaned. "Let it alone. You can't do any good."

George had already guessed what these men had to tell him. In a blazing flash of understanding Jesse remembered that other night when Rickart had unexpectedly come upon him and Blanche together; he realized, from the look of the man, that George must have seen more that night than he let on—had seen, or suspected, enough to prepare his mind for what he was hearing now.

Rickart said, in a weighted voice, "Go ahead, Lorn. What was it you saw?"

It was Shull who finished it: "Why, the pair of them, of course. Looked like they made a regular thing of it, too."

"No!" Blanche's heels tapped loudly as she went quickly to her husband's side. "It isn't so—not the way he makes it sound!" She clutched at his elbow, trying to make him turn and look at her. "You can't believe this!"

He was suddenly adamant, his voice expressionless. "Let go of my arm!"

"George!"

He did turn then. He jerked free of her grasp, and in front of all those men his hand swung and the flat palm of it struck her across the face—so hard that Blanche staggered.

Jesse's breath caught in his throat, but before he could have moved he felt someone close in behind him and the quick warning pressure of a gun muzzle, rammed against his side. Roy Shull, of course!

Not looking at anyone—at his wife or at the man who had been his foreman and intended partner in this ranch—George Rickart said slowly, "I didn't want to believe what I saw the other night, either, but a man can't shut his eyes forever!" He added, in a leaden voice, "Get your stuff together, Craven, and get off Broad R. Don't ever set foot on it again!"

Jesse recognized the finality of this. He knew the matter was ended as far as Rickart was concerned, and that there was nothing to be gained by explanations. Blanche stood with a hand pressed against her cheek, staring at her husband. A sag of tired resignation had come into Rickart's shoulders. Something had ended for Rickart, too, in this moment.

Turning, Jesse shouldered the gunman aside. Without a look to right or left, he pushed his way through that stunned room and walked out of the house.

With the lights of the Clevenger place before him, Jesse Craven hesitated, suddenly reluctant to stop here. He debated, even as he rode into the yard and halted, toying uncertainly with the reins as the buckskin shifted its hoofs under him.

He was ready to travel, his meagre accumulation of personal belongings built into a pack and strapped behind the cantle. Perhaps he ought to turn again and ride on—there would be questions, questions he couldn't answer with Catherine's eyes studying him, their cool glance probing behind his words.

And yet, he couldn't go without asking about Dave Clevenger.

Nearly every window of the house was lighted, but in the front bedroom the lamp burned dim behind carefully drawn shades. As Jesse looked at those windows the front door opened and a puncher came hurrying out and down the steps on some errand. Jesse leaned forward to ask anxiously, "How's your boss?" The cowboy shot him a look and was gone without answering. A moment longer Jesse hesitated: then he swung down and, leaving the reins trailing, mounted the steps to the door.

He knocked softly at first, waited a moment and tried again; he was about to turn away, not wanting to disturb the people within, when through the glass he saw Catherine coming from the sick room. A wall lamp showed the strain she was under, the tightness about her mouth and a kind of desperation that stained her eyes and made them seem darker. When she opened the door and saw Jesse, she merely stood with her hand on the door and for a moment seemed not even to recognize him; that, he knew, was the preoccupation with her father's illness.

Hat in hand, Jesse said, "I'm leaving. I thought I'd drop by and see how Dave was doing—if there was any change."

He thought her eyes widened a trifle, her mouth slackening. She moved her lips before her voice came, faint and not sounding like her own. "Come in, please."

Paul Talbot stood in the door of Dave Clevenger's room, which opened to the left directly off the hall. He was coatless, his sleeves rolled up, and fatigue showed in his eyes. He greeted Jesse with a nod and stood aside as the other man walked in and stood at the foot of the bed looking down at the unconscious figure of the rancher.

In the shaded light, Dave Clevenger's face appeared waxen and old; it startled Jesse, who had never thought of Dave as being anything but in the prime of life. He watched the uncertain breathing that lifted the bandaged chest. There was a hard constriction in his throat, suddenly; it was work to swallow. He lifted his glance to Paul Talbot and their eyes met, above the girl's bent head; the doctor's sober shake of the head told Jesse all he needed to know.

Numbed by grief, he turned and walked woodenly out of the room. He had nearly reached the front door when Catherine's question sounded behind him. "What—what was it you said about leaving?"

He came around slowly, to discover that she had followed him. Taller than most girls, she yet had to tip her head back as she looked anxiously into his face; the pallor of her skin made the raven-black hair seem even darker in the yellow spray of light from the wall lamp.

Jesse said, briefly, "George Rickart and I had sort of a flare-up, and that's the way it ended."

Paul Talbot had appeared in the hallway behind Catherine. "Are you leaving the country?" he demanded. "For good?"

"I don't know. Appears like it."

But Catherine said, suddenly, "Wait!" and as he turned she indicated the archway to the living room. "Come in here, Jesse—where we can talk!" He hesitated briefly before he followed. She walked directly to the round center table, where the ornamental lamp with the frosted glass shade stood, and swung around to face him. Jesse's eyes fed on her beauty as he joined her.

The doctor had halted in the archway, where he could hear any sound that might come from Dave Clevenger in the room across the hall.

"Now," said Catherine, with firmness in her tone. "Just what happened at Rickart's?"

"If you don't mind," Jesse told her, "I'd rather not talk about it. It was a—a misunderstanding, as a matter of fact. But it made things so I couldn't stay. I'm pulling out."

"What about your people on the bench?"

Jesse frowned. "That's the hard part," he admitted. "Looks like trouble brewing for them with the whole valley, and if it does come they'll need me." He spread his hands. "I've been away so long," he added, lamely, "I doubt whether there's really any place for me up there—whether I could fit in now, or would even want to."

"I think you're right," Paul Talbot said, nodding. "You've outgrown them, Jesse. You're too big for that life; you wouldn't be happy."

"Doesn't look much as though I belong anywhere, after the showing I made at Broad R!"

Catherine said, on a note of warm compassion that startled him and brought his eyes to her in wonder, "You're bitter, Jesse, because you've been hurt badly! I'm sorry."

"I'm not asking for sympathy!" He felt the hot tide of humiliation begin to rise into his throat and face; suddenly he was so acutely uncomfortable that he wanted only to be away from there, and he mumbled, "Thanks, anyway, to both of you. I hope Dave gets better fast!" He snatched up his hat, but he hadn't got more than a step or two toward the hall when Catherine's cry halted him.

"Jesse! Wait!"

It turned him back; she had dropped her cool manner of assurance enough to come a step after him, a hand raised. Jesse saw a look pass swiftly between the girl and the doctor.

Paul Talbot nodded. "Are you thinking what I am, Catherine? I do believe you are!"

"Thinking what?" Jesse looked from one to the other in puzzlement.

"That it would be a mistake to let you go! Rickart's loss can be the Clevengers' gain! Catherine, even if your father recovers, it will be a long time before he can sit a saddle. And with roundup in progress, you're going to need a foreman to run things—the best man you can find. I think you've got him right here!"

Jesse could only stare, as he realized the man was serious. He swallowed once, and blurted, "You're not serious!"

"I admit I'm no cattleman—but I know a man when I see him!" Talbot turned to the girl. "If an outsider can be allowed to make a suggestion, I think you'd better grab Jesse while you have the chance!" After that, as though he felt he had said all he should, he turned abruptly and walked out of the room.

Then Catherine asked, in a strangely breathless voice, "Will you, Jesse? Stay and work for me?"

He turned slowly and came back. He stood close to her, and the upwash of light from the table lamp showed him her face, more lovely than he had imagined in many lonely nights in his bunk at Broad R. He forced down the impulse to touch the warm ivory of her lifted throat, and in an unsteady voice said, "You don't really mean that, Catherine! Just because Doc—"

"My mind was made up," she answered simply, "before he spoke. I've got a loyal bunkhouse crew, but no one I could feel the same kind of confidence in that I could in you, Jesse."

He shook his head a little. "I just don't savvy. To tell you the truth, I never thought you had any use for me at all."

Her eyes fell before his own searching gaze; it was the first time he had ever cracked her manner of sure coolness.

When she answered her voice was small. She spoke with an effort and all her poise was gone. "I know what you mean. I'm afraid I haven't been very friendly. But a person can't always help herself. I do like you, Jesse. I always have. The truth is I've always been a little—afraid of you!"

"Afraid?"

She nodded; he could see only the top of her head, the shine of the lamp running across its black richness. "From the time we were children, and you came down off the bench every day on that funny, one-eared mule. You were so different from the rest of us."

"Like my people, you mean?" He shrugged. "It was just a bluff, mostly—trying to cover how scared I really was. You all plagued the very life out of me!"

Her head came up. "Oh, Jesse! I didn't mean it! I'm sorry—truly I am!" There was complete sincerity in her, and when incredulously he took her hand, her fingers closed warmly on his. "Will you stay, Jesse?"

He dropped her hand, abruptly. "Have you thought what Rickart's going to say? How will he take having me ride for you on the roundup? Having to work with me, after what's just happened?"

"I see." The light died in her eyes as quickly as it had been born. "Of course, you're right. I didn't intend to be selfish, thinking only of myself. It would be an impossible position for you."

"That isn't the idea. Far as I'm concerned I could stand up to any of them and not give a damn what they thought. But—" He deliberately roughened his voice. What he had to say must be said bluntly; there was no other way. "You'll find out eventually why I was fired, so I'll tell you: It was because of Blanche!"

"You don't mean—"

Jesse saw the shocked understanding and then the hurt that came into her face. "It wasn't true. But George thought—Well, it don't matter what he thought, but can't you see? It wouldn't be long before Rickart and Mathison and the others might be starting worse talk. About me and you, Catherine! And I can't have that happen!"

She looked into his determined face. "I wouldn't care!" she answered him. "It wouldn't matter one bit, if you'd just say you're willing to stay on!"

"But—" Argument died before the earnestness of her plea, the astonishing change in her. Jesse knew suddenly that he was seeing her as she really was. The cold aloofness that had always dismayed and rendered him tongue-tied was no more than a pose.

Afraid of him! How long it had taken him to learn the truth—tonight, when it might have been too late to find out what she really was like.

He swallowed the refusal he couldn't speak, and slowly nodded.

"All right, Catherine," he said, solemnly. "If you really mean it, I'll be proud to stay on."

Chapter Fifteen

Later he stood alone on the porch listening to the night wind and the subdued sounds of the ranch, and watching a spreading fan of silver that heralded a full moon. In his thoughts he was reaching ahead to tomorrow and the days that would follow, to what would happen when the Clevengers' neighbors learned that he was now the C Cross foreman.

Supposing Dave Clevenger lost his battle for life?

He wouldn't let himself think of that. It was worry enough that something might happen to make Catherine regret her decision, and her faith in him. Thanks to her, and to Doc Talbot, he'd gained a new place for himself when it had looked as though the loss of his job at Broad R had put him back at the foot of the ladder.

Today's events, with its thwarted manhunt, had brought the trouble between valley and bench to a crisis. The lid could blow off at any time; and if it did, Jesse would be caught in the middle, and so would the people he worked for. He didn't want to be the source of further grief to Catherine and her father, but if it came to an open fight he'd have no choice. He couldn't turn from his family on the bench.

Troubled by these thoughts and wondering if he'd done the right thing in promising to stay, Jesse dropped down the steps and took the reins of his buckskin, to lead it to the corral. He did not know why tension was in him, but with his gear and saddle stripped and his tired bronc turned into the pen, he found himself with rope in hand, building a loop to rope out a fresh mount and saddle it.

Standing there, he heard a single rider pressing in upon the ranch. He knew then that the instinct had been right, and this was the trouble he had been half consciously waiting for.

The moon had tipped above the high ridges and its leaf-shadowed light lay frosty over the yard. Jesse could see the horseman as a black silhouette, galloping through the high gate, and he must have been plainly visible himself because the man, without slowing, swerved directly toward him. Over at the bunkhouse a door was thrown open and someone stepped out to yell a curious challenge, but the rider didn't swerve. He pulled in beside the corral as dust, silvered by the moon, swirled about his horse's hoofs.

"Mister," he demanded breathlessly, "have you seen anything of—" He broke off in surprise. "Jesse! That you?"

Jesse Craven moved nearer, taking the bridle to help settle the sweating horse. "What's the matter, Tom? You looking for me?"

"I was sure hoping it wouldn't be too late!" Tom Nealy's voice shook with real relief. "You told me you'd be stopping off here, to see about Dave. I took the chance you hadn't left yet."

"What is it? Something wrong at Broad R?"

"Jesse, you weren't gone ten minutes when Rickart called me in and began pumping me about what happened at your folks' place today. Shull had been talking—I think he only waited for you to leave before he opened up. He'd told Rickart and Mathison and the rest that he trailed Dade Haggis there, and that you and me stepped in just as Shull was about to grab him."

A welling of fury roiled through the other man, hearing this. "And what did you say?" he demanded.

"Why, I told 'em exactly what happened. I told 'em I didn't see no sign of Haggis or anybody else. But Shull said he hung around and made sure for a fact they were hiding in your dad's loft, layin' up there and waitin' till one of the bunch is able to ride."

"He's a liar!" Jesse cried; but the moment the words were out, he knew it could be true. Hard as it was to think that his folks would deceive him, he had to admit a lot of distance had come between them in the time since he left the bench for good. Maybe they thought of him now as belonging to the basin, and for that reason some false idea of loyalty could have persuaded them to take in a renegade like Dade Haggis, and then not tell him.

But then he remembered that Tom Nealy had been with him, and instantly he felt a little better. Naturally, they wouldn't have dared speak out in front of Tom.

"Lorn Mathison's really ridin' a high saddle," Nealy was saying. "He's got the rest of 'em convinced and when I left they were about primed to ride up to your dad's place and take those bank thieves—over gunsights if necessary!"

"They do, and it'll mean shootin'! They're damn fools if they don't know the Cravens well enough to see that!"

Nealy retorted, "What of it? Isn't this what Mathison's been wanting all along? I did my best to argue, but George Rickart finally said either get ready to ride with the rest of 'em, or draw my time. You know I wouldn't have no part of what they're planning. I'm pullin' freight!"

He shook his head, his face unreadable under the shadow of his wide hat, his voice bitter. "Hell, I rode five years with that outfit—for Rickart, and his old man before him. But after what I seen and heard at Broad R tonight, I don't think I got any stomach left for Buel Creek people. That damned, bloodthirsty Mathison! And Shull—"

"Don't judge them all by that pair," Jesse told him. "Mathison isn't quite sane, and his gunman's a dirty killer. The rest are all right, without those two to stir them up."

"Will you still say that, if they ride up to the bench and burn your folks' place—maybe kill some of them?"

The question stopped Jesse for a moment; then he said gruffly, "The Cravens aren't that easy to kill!" He stepped back, giving his friend a slap on the knee. "Thanks a lot, Tom, for bringing me warning. Dunno what I can do to stop this, but I'll do something!"

"I wish you luck," grunted the puncher, without conviction, and lifted the reins.

"You're really leaving?" Jesse asked. "I wish you'd stick around, Tom. Buel Creek's your home. Maybe the Clevengers could find a place for you, if I asked 'em."

Nealy shook his head. "Thanks, but I've had a bellyful of this country!"

Jesse watched him go, wishing he could hold him. A good enough man, Tom Nealy.

He opened the gate and walked into the corral, shaking out a loop. There were half a dozen horses in the corral, and by moonlight he selected a light-colored bay and paced it around the bars, finally dropping the rope on it. He led it out, talking all the time to quiet it, and when it had decided it didn't mind the unfamiliar smell of him Jesse proceeded to pile on the gear he'd stripped from the buckskin. His blanket roll and warbag he left stacked against a post of the corral. Tonight he wanted no extra weight.

He left the ranch behind, and lined out across the flat bottomlands heading for Rickart's at a hard and steady pace.

The moment he brought Broad R's lights into view, though, he guessed he was already too late. The yard looked empty, with no sign of the men and the staked horses that had crowded it an hour ago. There was the momentary hope that Mathison and Shull might have lost out, after all, and that the crowd had dispersed, but he really hadn't any faith in this, and he hit the yard without slackening pace. At the house, a yank of the reins brought his mount to a blowing halt and he poised there, indecisive, seeing no movement against the lighted windows.

He gritted his teeth and was settling into the stirrups again when the door was thrown open and someone hurried out to the porch. It was Blanche; he might have spurred the bay, anyhow, except that something in the way she cried his name made him hold back, turning reluctantly. "Jesse!" She stood with one hand clutching a pillar, the other reached out to him. Lamplight behind her showed her blonde hair in disarray, and there was a wild note in her voice he'd never heard before. Astonished, he heard her exclaim: "You came back for me!"

"Mathison, and Rickart," he demanded impatiently. "They've gone?"

"The coward!" she spat, hearing her husband's name. "He hit me! In front of them all. He struck me, just as if I were a—were a—"

"I know, Blanche. George must have gone out of his head. He's the kind that bottles up and then suddenly explodes." Impulsively, he reached a hand across the railing to seize her arm. "Will you answer my question? When did they leave?"

Her voice shook; her flesh was cold to his touch, with the muscles hard and taut beneath the skin. "To think he would dare to raise his hand against me!"

Exasperated, Jesse shook her. "Are you listening?

They've gone up there, haven't they—up to the bench? I want to know how long it's been."

"I don't know." He must have got through to her. Her voice had lost its fever and her arm went limp. "A few minutes."

"Then maybe I've got a chance to beat them!" His mind was already miles away, sorting out the well remembered trails up the broken scarp.

"You didn't come back to get me? To take me away from this place?" Blanche sounded incredulous.

He answered impatiently. "All in the world I'm trying to do is prevent a war! For the sake of my folks, and for the valley too. Can you understand? If somebody doesn't do something there'll be a massacre, and it won't be only the bench people that get killed! Those men know how to scrap, and they'll be on their own ground. Mathison and Rickart are fools to have forgotten that!"

"Jesse!" Her voice had turned suddenly vibrant, with the idea that had seized her. The impetus of it carried her down the steps, to clutch at his knee. "Just as you said, up there anything could happen! George has treated you like dirt. If he should—if he didn't come back, then this ranch would belong to me. To us, Jesse! There'd be more for you than partnership. I'd give it all to you, Jesse—and myself with it!"

Gone cold inside, he looked down at her face that was strained and somehow not at all beautiful in the white mask of moonlight.

"Do you understand what I'm saying, Jesse?"

"Yeah," he grunted, not moving, not touching her. "Yeah, I understand. Well, don't worry! If I see George I'll send him back, whole, to his loving wife. That should be punishment enough for anything he ever did!"

He heard the sibilant intake of breath, saw her jerk away as though she'd been struck. Her lips moved and in a hoarse whisper the words hit at him: "You—you scum!"

His mouth twisted. "Thanks," he said, and lifted his hat to her.

With no other word he slammed the spurs home. He rode out and left her standing staring after him.

The moon ranged high, flooding the sky with its brightness and blanking out the nearer stars. Presently the ground began to break and lift under Jesse's running horse. In a mist of moonlight, the fault scarp that formed the bench reared dead ahead, seven hundred feet of naked rock deep scored through ages of erosion. Jesse Craven knew every ravine, every route by which cattle from the bench sometimes drifted down to the better graze below. He'd already chosen the shortest of these in his mind and now he pointed for it with a sure precision. The valley men, he knew, would be somewhere to the north of him, following the easier but longer loop that the main trail used.

It ought to give him a bare margin of time.

When he reached the ravine he was looking for he stopped for a moment to let his horse have a blow, and then pushed on. Here water and wind had cut deeply into the rock, forming a twisting and narrowing wedge. The moonlight didn't reach here; it made uneasy footing out of the shifting rubble of erosion. Grit, carried by the wind that siphoned down at him, stung Jesse's face and filled his eyes. Then as the pitch of the ravine became steep, he jumped down and led his horse.

The climb quickly leveled off again, and he was once more in the saddle. The rough walls fell back; he rode out onto the broken bench floor, where moonlight silvered scrub cedar and scattered pine, and the soil was so thin that his hoofbeats drummed on bare rock as he set the bay, without a pause, straight in the direction of the Craven holdings.

Beginning to draw near, he found himself holding his breath and listening for a sound of guns or horses running in the night; but except for the hoot of an owl somewhere in the trees behind his father's place the silence was complete. Apprehension gave way momentarily as he topped the last ridge and saw the lights of the house shining through the pines.

It looked as though he'd made it—but there wasn't much time.

He clucked to his jaded mount and eased down the slope, the horse shed just ahead of him as he came in from the south. Once he thought he heard movement off to his right and he was on such a nervous tether that he unintentionally jerked the reins; the hand that fumbled at his belt gun was clammy wet, and though he cursed himself and rode on, the nervousness stayed with him.

Coming out of the trees, he had a distinct sensation that, natural as the clearing and the buildings looked, the impression was false. There was something here that didn't feel quite right.

The feeling was so strong that when he reached the barn he rode up alongside and at the forward corner dismounted, to take a closer look over the yard to the house and try to sort out his disturbed thoughts. He was standing there when the sound of a snapped twig at his back made him turn sharply. In the seep of moonlight he could just see the two who'd stepped out from around the end of the barn. As he moved they halted. There was a click, and the faint gleam that a revolver barrel made.

His own weapon half out of holster, he caught the hoarse whisper: "Who is it?"

And his brother Homer's voice exclaimed, aloud: "Hell, I think it's Jess!"

They were beside him, then, and he saw that the second man was one of their bench neighbors, the oldest Means boy. Dry-mouthed from reaction, Jesse demanded, "What's going on here? What are you two doing prowling around this way—and why those guns?"

Homer told him, in a voice that was drawn hard with nerves: "We got word we may have visitors some time tonight—looks like the basin ranchers are planning to raid us! They try it and we'll sure give 'em more than they look for!"

"Maybe this boy knows something about it," the second man suggested darkly; Jesse could almost feel the suspicious eyes boring into him. "Maybe he's even leadin' 'em in! He sure sneaked past the guards we put out. . . ."

"I don't see any guards!" Jesse snapped. "And there's nobody with me. What do you mean by that? You talk as if I was a traitor!"

"Well, ain't you? Seems to me you sold us all out for the basin a long time ago; figured we wasn't good enough for you."

"That isn't so!" cried Homer, indignantly. "Why, Jesse never did feel like—"

"Let it go!" Jesse cut in. "Time's running too short for argument. You're right about the raid! Mathison's finally got what he's been yelling for, and the ranchers are on their way now. It's Dade Haggis they want. They claim he's laying up here."

Homer said, "They're mistaken!"

"I kept trying to tell 'em so, but nobody'd listen. I knew

you folks wouldn't have anything to do with a skunk like Dade after what happened in town!"

"Jesse—" Something in Homer's voice made the younger man look at him sharply. "In a way, they're right," his brother admitted. "It's true Dade's not here right now. But he was, earlier."

Jesse felt a sour numbness churn through him. "When Shull and his men came? And I stopped them from looking? Is that what you're telling me? You mean that they were here all the time?"

The other nodded. Jesse couldn't see his face. "We wanted to let you know, but never had a chance. . . . Dade and that skinny one he calls Arch Suttle rode in askin' for help, Suttle with this hurt leg—it was pretty bad, though they wouldn't say where or how he got it. And while Ma was fixin' it up, Shull and them others come lookin' for 'em.

"Naturally, whatever the trouble was we weren't gonna turn them out for Shull to murder. We put 'em in the loft, and then got rid of 'em as soon as we could after the Spade Bit men were gone."

"I see."

What Homer told him did give a little different angle. He thought he understood how it could have happened, but that didn't change the situation now. "Shull must have found out, just the same," he said. "And so, on account of Dade and that other no-good trash, you're all in bad trouble!"

"You got to give Dade some credit," his brother insisted. "It was him tipped us off about the raid tonight. I don't just know how he learned it was comin'—he said something about running across a man he knew in Mathison's outfit, who warned him. Anyway, he sneaked right back and let us know, so we had plenty of time to round up the boys and get set for it."

"But I don't savvy!" Jesse stared at his brother, while the night wind creaked the swaying treeheads behind the barn. "Dade's got no friends at Spade Bit! And even if he did, the only one might have had any inkling about this, ahead of time, would have been—"

Shull!

The idea hit him with a solid force. Incredible as it seemed at first, when he stopped to look back it was perfectly clear the raid tonight had been all Shull's doing, and it must have been deliberate. First, he'd worked adroitly to get Jesse out of the way so he couldn't interfere; after that it had been a matter of playing on Mathison and Rickart and the others, and whipping them up to this. Shull must have had some motive and plan that Jesse couldn't guess.

And why in the name of common sense would he have tipped his hand to Dade Haggis?

Plagued by questions he couldn't answer, Jesse shook his head impatiently and demanded, "Where's Pa? I want to talk to him."

"In the house," Homer told him. "Say, we got men and guns staked out all over the place, and in the timber. Even Rig Means left his fiddle at home and brought along his old breechloader. We're good and ready! Anyone who rides in here is gonna wish he—"

Jesse didn't stay to hear him finish. Leaving his lathered horse, he was already moving at a run across the yard, spurred by anxiety and by his sense of hurrying time.

Whether talking to old Bob would do any good, he didn't know; but if someone didn't prevent it, it seemed plain that something disastrous was about to happen here. Before, he'd been concerned about his own people. Now he knew that they were in no great danger, and that having been forewarned they could take care of themselves. But the basin men! They'd ride in, never looking for a trap, and with that moonlight to make clear targets for the bench guns it was not likely that many of them would ride out again.

Perhaps they didn't deserve any better! Apparently it wasn't any more than they, in their turn, had planned to do to Jesse's people. Still, murder was murder and it had to be prevented.

Just short of the house, his thoughts broke as something caught his glance and lifted it to the shallow ridge just north of the clearing. There was a gap in the feathery fringe of dark pine, where the town trail crossed. And what Jesse had seen was the silhouette of a rider lifting into view there, pausing a moment against the pale notch of sky. A second figure joined it. Then both dropped out of sight down the near slope, and others instantly replaced them.

Jesse knew then that he was too late. In the few seconds that remained he reached the house.

Chapter Sixteen

Lorn Mathison hauled rein for just that instant, studying the scene that the trail had opened below him. He'd never actually been this near the Craven outfit, and there wasn't a great deal he could tell about it in this uncertain light. It looked like a typical bench place—a house and a shed or two, and that was about all. Lamplight glowed in the windows, yellow and scarcely brighter than the white glow of the moon. An occasional spark rose lazily from the chimney, to be whipped away as the wind caught it up. The pines loomed black on the ridges, and somewhere at Mathison's right a dead snag creaked slowly, like a barn door that needed oiling.

That was when he first realized that Roy Shull was no longer at his side. Puzzled and vaguely alarmed, Mathison stood in the stirrups and twisted around, looking for him. The other horsemen, drawing in behind him, made the trail alive with moving shadows and glints of reflected moonglow—but he didn't see Shull, although they'd been stirrup to stirrup only moments ago.

Mathison scowled. He swung a probing glance into the timber at the side of the trail; then his eye jerked back as he glimpsed something. "Roy?" he demanded.

For some unknown reason, Shull had drawn back into the black pine shadows; it seemed almost with reluctance that he kneed his bronc forward. "Yeah?" he grunted, in a sullen tone. "Right here, boss."

"What the hell are you doing?"

"Thought I saw something."

Somehow Mathison didn't believe him, but he didn't know what else to make of the man's behavior. Meanwhile the rest of the cavalcade was close on them, and in the press of other things he let his questions go. Excitement throbbed along his nerves as he slipped the long-barreled gun from his holster. He repeated for Shull the instructions he had already given a dozen times.

"We go right in and take them by surprise, before they know what's happening. Haggis and the men that rode with him we want dead or alive; for the rest, there'll be no killing. But we're going to clean them out. All of them!

"They hold no legal title to this land. We'll let them take their horses and anything they can carry, and after that we'll burn their shacks and slaughter their scrub cattle so they won't have a chance to infect decent range. We do a fast, clean job and the law will never bother us. And then, by hell, we'll be rid of them!"

. . . Rid of these slovenly, shiftless people, whose very existence made a mockery of his whole way of life and the forty years of toil that had gone into it! Rid—he thought, his sunken eyes flashing—of their women—like Ellie Craven, whom he'd noticed on a summer day a year ago in Bueltown. He could remember still, with vivid clarity, her walking along in the hot sun as bold as brass, not even aware of the skimpy thinness of her cotton dress and the way it clung to her young body, of the enticing roundness of bare brown arms and legs, the swelling of a firm nubile bosom. He remembered himself standing transfixed, all thought of Spade Bit jarred from his mind—the ceaseless procession of stock quotations and tally figures and beef weights that made up the normal content of his thoughts all suddenly disrupted and broken.

He still grew hot as he thought of it! He, who scarcely knew when he last bothered to look at a woman, who was married only to his ranch and to his ambitions—in the very moment when he'd suddenly awakened to beauty and what he could have been missing, this Ellie Craven, this illiterate girl from the bench, had looked him in the face and passed on as though not even seeing him! For that humiliation, and for shaking him in his own sure estimate of himself and his values, Lorn Mathison had ever since hated her and all her people. He'd known that eventually they must be driven from this range so they could no longer taunt him for a wasted, fruitless existence . . .

He lifted the hand that held the gun, and brought his arm sharply forward. His shout released the men behind him. With a sudden jamming of spurs into horse flesh, the whole mob went pouring down the slope.

The buildings and the lamplit windows seemed to rush to meet them; the wind they made beat against slitted eyes and all but whipped the hats from their heads. Mathison had a momentary frightening vision of his horse losing its footing and of them both going down under that hurtling force of flesh and knife-sharp hoofs. But the moment passed. The bronc kept its feet, and now the ground abruptly leveled. They swept out into the open, the riders spreading out a little as they pressed in.

Less than a hundred yards from the buildings, Mathison's horse all at once swerved wildly when a heavy weight smashed into it broadside. Mathison thought his leg had been crushed against the stirrup fender. He cried out, sawing at the reins; and as his mount did almost a complete circle he glimpsed the rump of that other horse. Its rider had pulled it right around, making too sharp a turn in too small a space, and the impact with Mathison's horse had nearly thrown them both. Mathison, completely empty of thought in that jarring moment, glimpsed Roy Shull's face as the gunman threw his weight to one side to help gain balance, then straightened in saddle and jammed the spurs home.

Shull's horse bunched its legs and sprang at once into a violent run—but it had swapped ends and was pointing now toward the trail and the ridge they had just quit. Astonished, Mathison found his voice, but his shout was lost. A man reined wildly aside as Shull went hurtling past; a second failed to move fast enough and his horse took a glancing blow from the shoulder of Shull's mount and went down under him, squealing. But nothing stopped Shull. He was crouched forward in the saddle, like a jockey, raking his animal with the spurs while Mathison was left staring after him.

In that same instant, the lamp in the kitchen of the house was suddenly snuffed out.

It must have been a signal; for at the instant the light at the window vanished, the guns opened up. To Mathison's bewildered senses, there seemed to be a hundred of them. They let loose from every direction—from the house, from the shed, from the dark timber. Blinding flashes etched themselves on his vision as he swung about, trying to take in the size of the catastrophe. They were caught completely unprepared and completely helpless—perfect targets. And yet, even as Mathison lifted his six-shooter in a futile and belated effort to get in a shot, it occurred to him that the bullets were doing little damage.

He heard a cry that he thought was George Rickart's, as a horse somewhere close by reared and crashed heavily; but the only bullet that came anywhere near Mathison himself split the air some distance above his head. Dazed, he was wondering at this as he lifted his gun toward a small loft window, and threw a bullet at the smear of muzzle spark he'd seen there.

No one else seemed to have wits enough to return fire; his own shot came as an echo only to the fusillade of ambush, for the firing had died as quickly as it began. There was that one instant and then it was over, leaving concussion ringing in shocked ears, the squeal of terrified horses, the drifting stench of powder smoke.

Old Bob Craven's voice reached out to them: "You listen to what I got to say! That was just the first volley, to show you. The next one, we drop our sights and start emptying saddles. You can have it that way, or you can throw down your guns! Name it!"

Thwarted will had Mathison's jaws clamped so tight they ached. His eyes raked shadowed doors and windows, hunting the origin of that hated voice; but he sensed that the fight in his companions had been knocked out of them.

Stackpole, the last one to be talked into this enterprise, was the first to abandon it. His cry held a note of hysteria. "All right—all right! I'm throwin' mine away. For the love of God, don't shoot!" He spoke the literal truth; his arm swung high and his six-gun made a whirling streak of reflected light as he hurled it from him. It was a signal to the other men.

One or two at first, and then almost together, the guns began dropping from their hands and thudding to the ground about their nervous horses' hoofs. Only Mathison refused. Stubbornly holding to his weapon until the butt ground into his sweating palm, he glared his thwarted fury. Damn them! How could a man accomplish anything when he had to rely on the broken courage of fools? On cowards who could be turned back so easily from a task they'd set themselves?

Mocking him, old Bob's voice held triumph. "Glad to see you know when you're licked. Next time you figure to try a stunt like this, make sure there ain't no traitor in the deal to sell you out!"

Traitor?

Mathison's chest tightened as the word struck him. He knew instantly—he pictured Shull, drawing back just before the attack started; Shull, turning tail at the last instant before the lamp went out and the guns started firing.

Shull, for some dark reason of his own, had given he bench men warning so that this trap could be prepared and sprung, and then had played deserter at the showdown!

Fury whipped through Mathison; with it everything else —the other riders, even his enemies—was forgotten. He found himself sawing at the reins, jabbing steel into his horse as he yanked it around. There was a yell from men who pulled aside to let him through, but no shot came after him. All at once the way lay clear, and then he was heading for the timber at a hard gallop.

When the trail began to lift under him, a moment of reason returned. Shull had had several minutes start; he could be miles away by this time. But that was when he saw the motionless shape of horse and man, back at the edge of the trail.

A startled hand pulled the reins with such abruptness that the horse went to its haunches as it missed footing on a slick of pine needles. The animal caught itself, the wind tossed a branch aside, and moonlight swept across the face of the man on the other horse. It was Shull. Mathison realized as he brought up the gun he still held in his hand, that the traitor must have pulled in here to watch the springing of the trap.

Now they were suddenly face to face, and the cold breath of logic blew aside the last wisps of Mathison's fury. The gun was all at once too heavy a weight, and his trembling arm could not lift it quickly enough. Just as he brought it over, ready to fire, the horse sidestepped and threw him off balance, and he knew he was done for.

Shull's right hand moved, with no apparent effort. There was a searing explosion that blotted out Mathison's vision —a single, smashing impact, and then, nothing.

Jesse thought, afterward, that even if the others had understood the meaning of the shots up on the ridge, they were too wary of Roy Shull to do anything about it. But it didn't occur to Jesse to be scared. The shot acted as a signal that tore him loose from the place where he'd stood rooted during all this; it sent him on the run to his jaded horse, and put him into the saddle.

The bay didn't have much left, but it responded to Jesse's spurring. He swung wide, choosing to circle the back of the house where there would be no mass of startled horsemen to impede him, and afterward put the horse up the ridge at a long angle, designed to cut the trail at its top. As he rode through the trees, ducking branches, he thought he heard a quick flurry of hoofbeats across an outcrop somewhere above him. Then the pines fell back and, holding in for a moment, he glanced back downslope and saw the figure sprawled motionless in the trail. He knew it was Mathison; he didn't turn that way, but with a savage yank at the reins sent his horse pounding up the ridge.

If Shull wanted to make distance he would be bound to stick to the road, for a time at least; he wasn't too well acquainted with this bench country.

You couldn't read the mind of a man like that, but whatever Shull had meant to gain by his treachery, Jesse was willing to bet that what actually happened had been a disappointment. A swelling of pride filled him as he thought about it. It could have been a massacre, and old Bob and the rest would hardly have been to blame if they'd turned it into one. Instead, they'd gambled on meeting the danger without bloodshed, and they'd won.

Only one horse had been killed—George Rickart's saddler—and no man even scratched. Rickart wasn't hurt any; he'd be returning home, unscathed, to try to work out his problems with Blanche the best he could. The basin ranchers would have to change their ideas about the bench people when they realized that they'd probably all be dead except for the refusal of old Bob and his followers to turn this raid into a slaughter.

He topped the low comb of the ridge. Beyond lay an open stretch of thinly wooded area with a few scattered cedars and pine. The trail looped across this, and Jesse scanned it hurriedly, almost missing the pair of riders who'd pulled rein just below him, where the trail skirted a small patch of timber. The way they held their mounts on short tether, while the restless animals circled and kicked up a small film of moonbright dust, indicated that the pair didn't intend their meeting to last long. One was waving an arm excitedly, both men so engrossed that they didn't seem aware of Jesse. He came across the slope, holding back until he could discover who they were. At the thought that one might be Shull, his mouth had gone suddenly dry and his right hand was clamped tightly on the butt of his holstered gun.

He was still a couple hundred yards away when the one who had been arguing suddenly whirled his mount and went spurring straight across the moonlit flat. Something in that panicky haste warned Jesse; an instinct made him jab in the steel and prod his own tired bay to a run, as he jerked the six-shooter from his belt. Below him in the trail, there was a gleam of metal as the second man brought up a gun. Jesse saw the spurt of flame; a delayed instant later he heard the shot crack, flatly.

One bullet was all it took. The fleeing rider must have been hit hard between the shoulders, for he was thrown violently forward. He lost the stirrups and lost his seat; two more strides shook him loose and he went spilling down across the horse's shoulder. He twisted in mid-air, struck the ground upon his back and bounced once limply before coming to rest like a huge disjointed doll.

Horror tightened in Jesse. The cold-bloodedness of it, and the uncanny accuracy of the shooting, was all he needed to tell him who the killer was.

He started to kick the bay furiously; but next instant he knew, from an uncertain wavering that came into its stride, that his mount had done all it could. Tight-jawed, he pulled it in. Already the road ahead lay empty; Roy Shull had turned his mount and was gone again, disappearing past the tongue of trees and down a fall of the land. Pursuit being hopeless, Jesse reined to the right instead, and rode the few yards for a look at the man Shull had murdered. There, with the horse heaving and blowing between his legs, he sat for a long minute and stared at Dade Haggis—at blond hair blowing, at sightless eyes turned up to the moon.

A kind of sickness squeezed hard at Jesse's middle. Dade had been damned little use, but no one should end this way.

Jesse ran a palm slowly across his face, feeling the wiry beard that was starting to sprout. Nothing made sense—Dade's being here at all, or his connection with Shull, or the argument that had ended with him lying murdered on the ground. But there wasn't time for wondering.

The first warning that he was in danger came with the spat of a gun. Jesse's head jerked up so quickly that his hat tumbled off; the high white moon struck directly into his eyes. And squinting against it, he could see the two riders spurring out of the dark trees and coming straight at him.

Arch Suttle was in the lead. He had his bandaged leg thrust out grotesquely and an improvised crutch lashed to the saddle. The reins were in his left hand; a carbine rested across the forearm, his right hand at the grip. As he lifted the barrel and fired again Jesse heard the whine of the bullet.

Jesse brought up his handgun to answer the fire, at the same moment pulling rein to turn his fagged mount. Suttle came right on. He worked the lever and the carbine cracked again. Behind, the second rider was closing up.

Jesse held off the trigger and steeled himself to bear down, seeking a sure aim. That was when the carbine cracked a third time, and he felt the thud of the bullet striking meat. The bay gave an odd coughing noise, staggered once, and started to go down.

He had known instantly that the horse was mortally wounded; he was already shaking out of the stirrups and slapping a palm against the horn, levering himself for a violent sideward leap. He left the leather as the animal began falling. His boots struck the ground, hard. They slipped on slick, dry grass and the momentum of his leap carried him to his knees, with the horse rolling toward him. Past a tangle of legs and a flash of moonlight on polished shoe steel, he looked up at Arch Suttle as the saddletramp yanked to a sliding halt, almost spilling both horse and rider on top of the downed bay. They bulked huge and black, seeming to hang against moonwashed sky. And on the outline of Suttle's head and chest, Jesse deliberately put his bead, and squeezed his trigger.

He ducked, then, thinking the horse was going to leap right over him; but it veered, and as it went past he saw its saddle was empty and the stirrups flopping wildly. Jesse didn't even look to see Arch Suttle hit the ground. He was already turning his gun on that second rider. He didn't immediately recognize the shape of him, or the face that was shadowed by a wide-brimmed hat. But Jesse was on his feet now, half crouching behind the body of his horse. He gripped his gun, and threw his challenge.

"Hold it! I'm centered right on you, mister!"

Jesse felt little confidence that his challenge would have any effect. His hand was already tightening on the trigger, his whole body set for the gunfire he expected. To his surprise, this second man was suddenly hauling reins and his right hand swung up, empty. As braced hoofs spattered Jesse with dirt, the rider exclaimed, "I don't want none of this, Craven!"

"Then drop your gun," ordered Jesse. "Reach over with your left hand and do it." He didn't ease his careful attention, or let the six-gun waver. But the horseman didn't seem to want trouble. Right hand still raised, he groped across his body with the left, fumbled at his holstered gun and dropped it into the dirt.

As he did so his head lifted and surprise hit Jesse as moonlight showed him the coarse black hair, the dark features of Jim Pellman.

"This side of the pass just isn't healthy for you," he remarked dryly, straightening from the crouch his body had fallen into. His knees were suddenly shaky in the aftermath of the shooting. He kept his gun on the horse rancher; he didn't look at the body of the man he'd killed, or at Dade Haggis lying only a few feet away. "Don't you know there's a rope waiting for every man that had a part in the business this morning?"

He saw the breed's head jerk. "The holdup?" Pellman echoed. "You're wrong, Craven! I wasn't in on that!"

"These two were. How are you going to explain the fact you're here with them now?" Jesse's eyes narrowed, studying the dark face. "I think you may be telling the truth—but the basin men aren't apt to. If you don't want me turning you over to 'em, you better start talking."

Pellman hesitated. "If I do, you'll let me go?"

"That would depend on how straight you talk. And how fast," he added, thinking with impatience of Roy Shull getting farther away with every minute he wasted here.

"Sure." The horse trader shrugged. "Why not? It's all gone to hell anyway. Shull must have blamed Dade Haggis for the way their trap misfired, so Dade got a bullet."

"What were they after?"

"With the raid? Hell, it was supposed to be a slaughter. The reputation them bench people have for wildness, we figured with the ranchers under their guns they wouldn't hesitate a minute to blow the lot of 'em to pieces—instead of just shootin' over their heads!"

"But what would that have got Shull, and Dade?"

The other snorted. "With roundup half finished? Two thousand head and more of prime market beef gathered for the takin' and not enough valley men left alive to stop us takin' 'em if old Craven hadn't crossed us up."

Jesse was staggered. His swelling pride in old Bob was coupled with horror at the enormity of the thing Shull and Dade had planned, with the bench people for their unwitting tools. He wouldn't have thought even those two capable of anything quite that cold-blooded. And yet Blanche Rickart had tried to sell Jesse on making sure her husband didn't get back from the raid! It occurred to him, a little dazedly, that he was learning quite a lot about the human potential for evil, tonight. Blanche and Shull! What a team they'd have made. . . .

Pellman brought him back to the moment, saying anxiously, "You promised to let me go. You wouldn't let those basin ranchers come and catch me here?"

Jesse weighed the six-gun on his palm, considering. "You got any more men with you?"

"Three or four, all I could dig up on short notice."

"Take 'em and get out. And don't show your face this side of the pass again."

"It ain't likely!" muttered the breed. And when Jesse made no move to stop him he spun his horse and rode away. He didn't bother about the six-gun he'd dropped; he seemed glad enough to leave it behind.

Arch Suttle's knotheaded black hadn't traveled far after losing its rider, but it was still bothered by the shooting and it started a nervous sidling as Jesse came walking toward it, dragging on the hat he'd lost. He made a lunge and got the trailing reins before the animal could break away. It didn't look like much of a horse, but it would have to do. He ripped loose the makeshift crutch that Suttle had tied to the saddle strings, and tossed it aside. Then he swung into the saddle, reloaded, and took off.

One job remained to do—if it weren't already too late.

There would be no trailing Roy Shull, not even by moonlight as bright as this. Shull was finished in this part of the country; he knew it, and he wouldn't be wasting any time leaving it. And yet, knowing him for the man he was, it had struck Jesse that there was one final stop the gunman might try to make.

It was a long chance, but it was the only one.

Chapter Seventeen

SPADE BIT HAD THE LOOK of a place deserted. There was a faint glimmer of light in the cook's quarters, at the far end of the ranch yard; but no horses in the corrals, no life stirring. The main house was totally dark.

Almost convinced he'd guessed wrong, Jesse held up at a distance as disappointment settled in him. Then, because there was nothing else to do and he might at least make sure, he sent the black forward at a walk. As he rode in he checked the black shadows the moon threw down as it began tilting over into the westward half of the sky. There were places where a horse could have been tied and not be immediately visible. With the cook on the place, Shull would have to use precautions even if he didn't think it likely anyone from the bench would be quite this hot on his trail.

But when he had reached the house and found nothing, Jesse was about ready to give up. He was ready to lift the reins and turn his back on the whole futile business. when he saw something that caught and held him—the front door was open.

It might not mean anything, but it seemed unlikely a man as particular as Lorn Mathison would allow a door to be left standing wide, for stock and range predators to wander into an unguarded house. The hunch was so strong that it brought Jesse out of saddle to investigate. Dropping the reins, he went up and across the porch. There he paused for a moment, and pulled his gun. He stepped through the door and placed his back against the wall to one side of it, where he wouldn't form a silhouette; and then he stood and listened in pitch blackness.

He had been in this house just once, when he came by on some business with Rickart. Trying to place the layout, he thought again how typical of Mathison it had been to build something three times as big as he would ever need. To Jesse's left would be the door to the living room that had a fireplace big enough to stand up in. Opposite, against the wall, a staircase led up to the second floor, where there must be at least four bedrooms that were never used. Ahead and flanking the stairs a long hall led to the back of the house—to the kitchen that was seldom used either, since Mathison usually took his own meals with his crew and seldom had any guests to entertain. Back there, too, was the big room with its walls hung with deer and elk and pronghorn trophies—the room Mathison used most because it contained his desk and safe and all his records, and was the center from which he directed the business of this sprawling cattle ranch.

By contrast to the white world of moonlight outside, the

hall lay in utter darkness, the silence so profound that it seemed to pulse with the beat of his own heart.

Jesse was quite certain now that he was wasting his time. There was no one here but himself. Nevertheless, he pushed away from the wall and took a step forward; the chime of his own spur, dragging the floor, was startlingly loud. Jesse stopped, and with a grunt leaned to jerk the strap loose.

That saved his life. The shot, when it came, broke with heart-stopping suddenness in the cramped darkness of the hall, and the bullet passed somewhere above his bent shoulders.

Jesse dived prone to the floor, and hit rolling. He brought up on his right side with his back jammed against the bottom riser of the stairs. He lay there with his heart pounding and ears numbed by concussion, and felt the sweat flowing on him and the churn of his empty belly. At the back of the hallway, someone stood waiting to do it again, waiting to see if it was his first bullet that had sent the intruder sprawling. Now, as his hearing began to return to normal, Jesse thought he could hear the other breathing.

Shull? He knew suddenly that it had to be. A Spade Bit hand, defending his boss's property, wouldn't have lurked in the darkness; he wouldn't have loosed a bullet without at least singing out and challenging a prowler to identify himself.

Jesse's arm, and the hand that held his gun, had been trapped under him as he rolled. Now, very carefully, he lifted his body and slid the arm out from under, slowly extending it. He must have made some noise doing it, for there was a sharp exhalation of breath from the hall's end and then muzzle flash speared the darkness a second time, and a third. For a heartbeat the narrow hallway was brightened by the flashes—and Jesse had the barest glimpse of Roy Shull standing, ghostlike, behind the gun.

Rolling flat upon his belly, he shoved his gun arm straight in front of him and emptied his revolver, six rolling shots pouring their thunder into the muddled echoes.

He fired until the hammer clicking on spent cases told him the gun was empty. If none of those bullets had happened to tally he was helpless, now—but with that thought there came the sound of something slumping against the wall at the end of the passage, and then a confused shuffle of boots and the slow sliding of a body as it fell. Even after the loose thud of its hitting the floor, Jesse Craven could only lie where he was, fighting the churning of his stomach.

When he was over that, he set about reloading his gun.

He moved with caution, cursing the small noises he made; for he realized now that Shull was not yet dead. Breathing, labored and painful, filled the hallway; when Jesse stopped to listen he could hear a faint stirring back there. By the time Jesse had the last used shell replaced from his belt and the loading gate clicked shut, his clothing was drenched and he laid the gun down for a minute as he swabbed a sleeve across his face. He remembered his spurs and took a moment to slip them off. Afterward, pulling himself a little unsteadily to his feet and with his back flat against the bannister, he started moving cautiously ahead.

At once, the labored breathing stopped. He knew Shull had heard him and was holding his breath, waiting. It took nerve to keep himself moving, into the sightless darkness piled at the end of the corridor. A man could be badly wounded and yet able to use a gun; and it was even possible that Shull could see him against the moonlight filling the open door. He might only be waiting for his victim to get close enough to make a sure target.

Jesse halted finally. It was one of the hardest things he ever did, to fumble a match out of his pocket, hold it at arm's length while he summoned his nerve, and then snap the head against the edge of his thumbnail. The pop of the match was like a shot. The yellow flame sprang up; Jesse managed to keep his taut nerves from squeezing the trigger.

Shull lay crumpled on his side, jammed against the wall with his head canted hideously against it. One of Jesse's bullets had broken his leg, another had hit him in the chest. The blood was flowing freely, soaking both his clothing and the money that lay scattered around him, where the cashbox—rifled from Lorn Mathison's office desk—had spilled open as he fell.

There was blood on his lips. His eyes were glassy as he peered up at Jesse standing over him. Little life remained in those eyes, but there was hatred. And Shull's hand, lying limp on the bloody carpet beside him, fought now to raise the gun that it still held.

A mere nudge from Jesse's boot toe was enough to dislodge the weapon, and put it beyond the dying man's reach. Shull looked down at his empty fingers for a long time, as though failing to understand what had happened. Then the eyes lifted again to Jesse's face and the man's lips moved.

"I ought to have killed you," he said, so faintly the other could scarcely hear. "I misjudged you and them other Cravens. I thought—"

His face twisted. Jesse supposed pain had merely interrupted his speech; it was a long moment before he realized that the eyes were not seeing him any more, but were staring past and through him and into eternity.

The match twisted to a blackened curl and went out; darkness returned with a rush. Slowly Jesse eased the six-gun off cock with a hand that was cramped with tension. Outside he heard footsteps running and knew the Spade Bit cook must be on his way from the kitchen shack, at the far end of the yard.

Paul Talbot said, "You're a lucky man, Mathison. I wonder if you realize that? Just a quarter inch difference in the direction of that bullet. . . ."

Mathison's face, beneath the bandage that covered the top of his head, was waxen in the lamplight. His eyes flickered and he managed to say, "I know."

The doctor stepped back, with a nod to Ellie Craven. He saw the expression in the hurt rancher's eyes as the girl moved in to straighten the pillow and draw the covers tight; he saw the way Mathison's eyes followed her every movement. The rancher said, "Could I have some water?"

"I'll get it," Ellie said, and went out of the bedroom.

Talbot spoke again, unable to keep harshness out of his voice. "Perhaps it's no use, but I hope you've learned a lesson. After what you tried, to have these people take you in and give you this kind of care—" He shook his head. "You don't deserve it, Mathison!"

He stopped, then, seeing an expression he had never expected to find in this man's face. There was pleading in it, and humiliation. "Lay off, Doc!" the hurt man begged, hoarsely. "You can't tell me anything I haven't already told myself!" The grooved cheeks whitened over bunched muscles. "It isn't easy to face the fact you've been wrong! I never have before."

Before that abject surrender, the dislike Talbot had always felt toward this man slowly died, and pity took his place. He frowned and said gruffly, "You might start by saying you're sorry!"

Ellie returned, then, with a cup of water. Paul Talbot watched the gentleness with which she slipped an arm behind the hurt man's shoulders and helped him up, taking his weight against her while he drank. He left them like that, and went out into the main room of the house.

After all that had happened earlier, it seemed strangely silent. The basin men had ridden away an hour before; the bench people had scattered to their homes. Bob Craven and his wife were alone, sitting at the table while the fire in the stove made the only sound. Both old people looked up, quickly, as Talbot closed the door of the bedroom carefully.

"How's Mathison?" Bob asked, in a heavy tone.

"All right."

Talbot came slowly into the room. He had taken a cherrywood pipe from his pocket; as he examined the bowl he said, "Your daughter has made a conquest, I think! I don't know what she's done to him, but I've never seen such a change in a man. She's got him eating out of her hand." Looking at the man and woman, then, he added, "I think a good many things have changed tonight. They should all be better neighbors, after this."

"Let's hope so," grunted Bob, and got to his feet. Tonight he did look old, and spent, as though the things that had happened had taken their toll. He said, "I'll fetch up your horse. Homer and Billy ain't around to do it—they went looking for Jess."

"For Jesse?"

"Homer told us he was here when the ranchers came," Maud Craven explained. "But right after that he disappeared again. We're a little worried."

Talbot rubbed the bowl of his pipe with a thumb. "I wouldn't be."

Bob said, "We figure he may have gone after Roy Shull!"

The doctor considered this, frowning; but then he shook his head. "I still don't think I'd worry too much!"

"It'll be morning in a few hours," the woman said then, with an anxious look at the doctor's drawn face. "You look frazzled. Can't you stay, and get some rest until then?"

"Why, thanks," he said. "Perhaps I'd better. It's been

a strenuous day, and I think Dave Clevenger can get along without me for a few hours. He was resting well. I have an idea he's going to pull out of this, after all."

"I'm damned glad to hear it," old Bob exclaimed. "He's a good man, worth a dozen like Rickart and Mathison. But maybe they'll be easier to get along with after what we taught 'em tonight!"

Maud Craven suggested, "Why don't you try it in the loft, Doctor? Nobody'll disturb you there, and you can sleep as long as you like. If the boys get back we'll keep 'em out."

"I may take you up on that," Talbot agreed. "But, first, I'd like to get myself some fresh air, and try to unwind a little." He showed her the pipe. He was already reaching for his tobacco pouch as he started for the door.

The moon was nearly gone, now. Shadows stretched long across the yard ,and the stillness was profound. It was hard to believe there had been violence here a few short hours ago. Even George Rickart's dead saddle horse had been roped and hauled away by a couple of the Cravens' neighbors. As he walked slowly across the clearing and into the shadow of the trees, he felt the ground under his feet uneven and torn by many hoofs. That was the only reminder.

He filled and packed his pipe, tightened the drawstring on the leather pouch and dropped that into his pocket. The chill of autumn was strong tonight, he thought, as he placed the pipe in his mouth and dug out a match to light it with. He struck a light, then suddenly shook his head and blew it out. He threw the match aside and dropped the pipe, unlit, into his pocket.

Restless with the thoughts that crowded his mind, a smoke was not what he wanted. It was a measure of the things that troubled him, that his faithful pipe was suddenly unable to touch them. He shrugged, turning abruptly, and saw Ellie.

He hadn't heard the door opening, and near as he was to her he was certain Ellie hadn't noticed him in the shadows. She had thrown a dark shawl about her, against the night coldness, but her apron made a faint white gleam and his eyes could follow her as she moved along the side of the house. She seemed to walk with no more purpose than himself, and now she had stopped and put her back to the logs, and appeared to be looking up at the stars. Knowing he would have no peace of mind until he had spoken what needed to be said, he started walking toward her.

When he heard the sound of her crying, the resolution almost died in him. But he went ahead, and said quietly, so as not to startle her, "Ellen—"

Her gasp and quick turn toward him showed that she hadn't known of his approach. "Oh," she said, a little tremulously. "Is it you?"

"I don't want to intrude, and I'll go away if you ask me. But—" he summoned his courage— "I heard about—heard that they'd found your husband. I'm very sorry. For your sake I wish it could have been any other way."

She tried to answer, but the uncontrollable sobs came again and she turned away from him. Only an instant the man debated, and then he took another step and put his hands on her shoulders. At his touch she seemed to wilt, and made no protest as he turned her, gently. Next moment her head was pressed against him and she was sobbing on his shoulder.

"Dade wasn't any good," Ellie's muffled words came. "He just wasn't. It was bound to end like that."

"Perhaps. But that doesn't make any difference, I know. Nothing ever matters, really, when it's someone you love."

He felt the shake of her head. "I suppose I did love him, once; I don't know. It—it seems so long ago. But I'm not crying because of him."

Puzzled, Paul Talbot said, "But what is it, then?"

"It's my baby!" she answered, and went wholly to pieces. "To do this to him—before he's even born!" Sobs shook her.

For a long moment, not speaking, he let her cry out her despair. But then he asked the question circumstances had finally made possible.

"Will you marry me, Ellen?"

She went completely still, and then suddenly she was drawing back and he released her. Her face was a pale stain in the darkness as she looked up at him, trying to see his eyes.

"You—you don't know what you're saying!"

"What makes you say that? I've had it in mind for a long time. And it isn't pity!" he added quickly, before she could interrupt. "That's one word I won't let you use! I'd never ask you on any such basis, because I'm sure you wouldn't accept. I don't know what opinion you hold of me, or if you even have one. But I love you, Ellie," he finished gently.

Her voice sounded choked and incredulous. "How could you?"

"Love someone as strong as you, you mean? And gentle, and altogether fine? I've waited a long time for such a woman; I'll admit that this bench is the last place I'd have hoped to find her! But I suppose it isn't fair to ask you—right now—if you'll have me."

He saw her shake her head. "But you don't want—Dade's child!"

"Your child, Ellen—can't you understand? I would love anything that was part of you. All that matters is whether there's any chance you could come to feel anything of the kind for me!"

He held his hands rigidly at his sides. For a moment he thought she was not going to answer him at all; but then she tilted her head and her eyes were swimming, and it seemed that all the starlight in the sky had collected there to shine up at him.

"Oh, Paul!" she whispered. "How could I help it?"

It was well past midnight when Spade Bit crew came home, sobered and silent, and found Jesse Craven and Mathison's burly cook sitting in the kitchen shack sharing a pot of coffee. Jesse's holster was empty. His six-shooter was shoved behind the cook's waistband and a sawed-off twin-barreled shotgun lay across the latter's knees. The punchers crowded in, staring, and somebody exclaimed, "What the hell goes on?"

Jesse looked at them over the rim of his coffee cup. It was the cook who answered, with another question. "Craven, here, says that Roy Shull killed the boss. Is that true?"

"He didn't kill him," a puncher said. "But it wasn't for not tryin'! Shull led us all into a trap, and he shot Mathison and come within an ace of drillin' his skull. Then he got away."

Slowly, the cook turned and looked at Jess. "All right," he grunted. "I guess you told it straight; but it was damned hard to believe! Here's your gun." He brought it out and shoved it across the table, and Jesse put it in his holster. To the puzzled crew the cook said, gruffly, "Shull didn't get very far. He's lyin' over there in the house with a couple of bullets in him, probably cold by this time. I guess he must have been trying to clean out whatever cash he could find, when Craven caught up with him."

"Craven? He done for Roy Shull?" one of the men echoed, incredulous. "And you had the nerve to pull a gun on a man who could do that?"

The cook looked suddenly sheepish. Jesse, getting tiredly to his feet, told him, "It's all right. I couldn't blame you —you had only my word as to what had been going on. And I wanted to stick around, anyway, to learn the score on Mathison." He picked his hat off the back of his chair and drew it on. "I'll be riding. You really think your boss will live?"

"That's what the doc says," the first man told him. "They put him to bed at your folks' place until he's well enough to move." He hesitated. "I—it looks like there's been a lot of careless talk about those people on the bench, Craven. After all, they could have massacred the lot of us, if they'd been of a mind to."

Jesse said, shortly, "Thanks!" and walked out. The men drew back to make room, and he could feel their stares follow him. . . .

It still lacked an hour of dawn. Jesse rode slowly, too tired to fight speed from the knotheaded bronc under him. It was a dead man's saddle he forked, and it put him in mind again of all the men who had died since the sun last went up on this range: Pete Horn, Arch Suttle, Dade Haggis, Roy Shull. And Lorn Mathison and Dave Clevenger had both come within an ace of joining them! He shook his head. Did any good ever come from so much killing?

Might be, he supposed. If what had happened today had been enough to teach the men of the valley and the bench a little more about one another than they had known before, and make a better future possible for them both, then it was worth it. . . .

There was still the lamp, turned down low, behind the drawn shade of Dave Clevenger's bedroom, and that other one burning in the hall; otherwise everything at C Cross was dark and sleeping now. Jesse rode in past the darkened bunkhouse, and paused a moment before the house. He started to dismount, then shook his head and dropped back into the saddle; concerned though he was to know if Dave was better or worse, he did not feel like disturbing Catherine. She might be sleeping.

He took the reins again, and clucked to the horse. He was just riding on when he saw the shadow fall across the glass of the big door.

At once he hauled rein and was out of the saddle before the door could open. He went up the steps quickly, and then Catherine was on the veranda—a tall, slim figure in a belted robe, her dark hair falling loose and soft about her shoulders. The light from the door lay upon their faces; she seized his hands and looked up at him anxiously.

"Dave?" Jesse demanded, sharply.

She shook her head. "He's sleeping. I think he's going to be all right, Jesse. But you?"

"What about me?"

She spoke in a tumble of words and pent-up feelings. "One of the men saw someone come and talk to you, and he said you took a fresh horse and rode away in a hurry. I was sure something must have gone wrong. I knew it when word came from the bench that there'd been shooting and Paul Talbot was needed. I've—I've been so afraid!"

"Afraid for me?" he echoed, and remembering something she'd told him his mouth twisted suddenly into a smile. "Not afraid *of* me, this time?"

She didn't smile. Her hands tightened on his and she said, breathlessly, "All I knew, all at once, was that if anything happened to you—that if you didn't come back—"

"You ought to have known," said Jesse, "that nothing on earth could keep me away!"

And when he kissed her, she came warmly into his embrace.

THE END
of a novel by
D. B. Newton

D(wight) B(ennett) Newton is the author of a number of notable Western novels. Born in Kansas City, Missouri, Newton went on to complete work for a Master's degree in history at the University of Missouri. From the time he first discovered Max Brand in Street and Smith's *Western Story Magazine*, he knew he wanted to be an author of Western fiction. He began contributing Western stories and novelettes to the Red Circle group of Western pulp magazines published by Newsstand in the late 1930s. During the Second World War, Newton served in the U.S. Army Engineers and fell in love with the central Oregon region when stationed there. He would later become a permanent resident of that state and Oregon frequently serves as the locale for many of his finest novels. As a client of the August Lenniger Literary Agency, Newton found that every time he switched publishers he was given a different byline by his agent. This complicated his visibility. Yet in notable novels from *Range Boss* (1949), the first original novel ever published in a modern paperback edition, through his impressive list of titles for the Double D series from Doubleday, *The Oregon Rifles*, *Crooked River Canyon*, and *Disaster Creek* among them, he produced a very special kind of Western story. What makes it so special is the combination of characters who seem real and about whom a reader comes to care a great deal and Newton's fundamental humanity, his realization early on (perhaps because of his study of history) that little that happened in the West was ever simple but rather made desperately complicated through the conjunction of numerous opposed forces working at cross purposes. Yet, through all of the turmoil on the frontier, a basic human decency did emerge. It was this which made the American frontier experience so profoundly unique and which produced many of the remarkable human beings to be found in the world of Newton's Western fiction.